NOTHING SPOIL

a novel

KELVIN ALANEME

Ala Africa Books
Published by Ala Africa Inc.
Suite 9908, 1606 Headway Circle, Austin, Texas 78754, USA

USA | UK | Nigeria

NOTHING SPOIL

An Ala Africa Book / published by Ala Africa, Inc.

Printed in Nigeria by Libretto Publishers Ltd for Ala Africa Books.

ISBN: 979-8-9927448-1-1

This book is dedicated to all young Nigerian girls.

ACKNOWLEDGEMENTS

This book has been twelve years in the making. First, I want to appreciate a young lady, whose name I can no longer remember. The story she told me and her permission to share it with the world under anonymity formed the foundation of this book.

I want to thank my Facebook friends who read the initial parts of the story in 2013 as I posted it, and who craved for more, even when I told them that the story was over. "What became of Stella?" they would ask me on random posts. I hope this book provides you with the closure that you have been seeking for over a decade.

Special thanks to my editors - Emem Alexandra Akpan-Nya and Hannu Afere - who worked on the manuscript, sharing useful insights as we beat the story into shape.

To my family and colleagues who have been part of this journey - supporting me and cheering me on, thank you.

Last, I thank Rita and my lovely children - Zikora, Olisa and Zobam - whose warmth, support and succour ensured that this story saw the light of day. I love you.

ONE

July 25, 2006.

I've always seen my life as one big drama whose drunk director took pleasure in pushing me to the edge. But nothing prepared me for what was to come.

That evening, the sky was pregnant with grey clouds. My palm itched and I stood there, scratching until I had relieved myself of the sensation. People said it meant something big was on its way. Money, good luck or something else. But I wasn't one given to superstition.

All that has changed now.

TWO

In the streets, a strong wind wreaked havoc. People rushed to their clotheslines to clear laundry. Children previously playing a spirited game of catcher, packed up their slippers and hurried indoors.

A fair-complexioned girl walking past my shop shrieked, as the breeze blew her gown upwards. Underneath the gown, a flash of pink panties and thick dark thighs made on-lookers roar with laughter. She struggled to hold it down and scurried away, embarrassed.

"No dey bleach, una no go hear!" a man shouted from across the street. Some men leered as they put away their unfinished game of draughts. Loud mouths.

I was closing my shop, when a young man approached me. He had a travelling bag slung over his shoulder.

"Madam," he said. "Please, I just arrived in Lagos and I am stranded. I lost my wallet with my money and the address of my contact at Ore. My phone is dead. I really need a place to spend the night and sort myself out."

His deep voice was soaked in desperation. A drop of rain landed on his nose as he spoke and we looked up at the gathering clouds.

I wasn't one to be swayed by sob stories. However, there was something in the manner he asked that was different. He didn't lurk around the shop, trying to make up his mind on who to approach. He had walked straight to me.

It began to drizzle. He moved out of the rain, taking shelter under the zinc roof in front of the shop. Tears formed at the corners of his eyes as he awaited my response, his shoulders squared as though braced for uncertainty.

His story wasn't uncommon. Tales abound of young people who left their villages for big cities like Lagos, in search of a better life. Many ended up sleeping under the bridge till they found their feet. I was like him once. My saving grace was a relative who housed and fed me till I became independent.

Raindrops pelted the roof, their increasing frequency warning us of an imminent downpour. I needed to get home fast or I would be stuck as I wasn't with an umbrella. What could go wrong with housing someone for a night?

"Look, the rain is coming. My house is close. I can only shelter you for one night."

He fell to his knees. "Thank you. Thank you. I will be gone in the morning."

I cut short his effusive display of gratitude, helping him to his feet. "I'm Stella."

He shook my outstretched hand. "Jidechukwu Onuwa. You can call me Jide."

We walked into the gathering rain.

THREE

My house was at the end of the street. A two-storey building, surrounded by a fence with pieces of broken bottles sticking out the top, the landlord's attempt at discouraging petty thieves.

Mama Tunde's children were defying the rain and still kicking a leather ball around. The dirty-brown thing made its way towards our direction and Jide trapped it with his left foot, sending it back in a practiced shot. They cheered and then paused the game to let us pass, shouting their excited greetings after us.

"Aunty Stella, good evening! Uncle, good evening!"

We responded, and then made our way up the dark stairs to the first floor where I lived.

There was no power supply and the room was stuffy, so I opened the louvres, slightly, to let fresh air in. The rain showed no signs of abating.

"Welcome to my home," I said, as I took Jide's bag from him. "Please make yourself comfortable."

He relaxed on one of the sofas and looked around, a smile forming around his lips. "You own this place?"

"Yes," I chuckled at the mix of wonder and admiration in his voice. I carried his bag into the room and then headed to the kitchen to prepare dinner.

I wondered if he was bored, and prayed that the power supply would be restored so he could entertain himself with the television. But by the time I was done cooking, my prayer remained unanswered; the house was still dark, and only the sound of the rain broke the silence.

Over yam and beans porridge, I profiled him in my head. He ate with his left hand and appeared shy at first but became livelier with each forkful.

"Please eat well," I said, my eyes moving from his handsome features and sparse beard, to his mouth as he chewed. "Tomorrow, you can resume the search for your friend's place."

That night, I learnt that he was twenty-eight with two younger siblings and a widowed mother. He had come to Lagos from Aba in search of greener pastures, having undergone some apprenticeship with a tailor. He had absconded just a year before the agreed three years of training, on account of maltreatment.

"Do you always quit things halfway?" I asked.

He appeared shaken by my question. "If it were only the nightly flogging with his belt, maybe I would have endured one more year." His eyes became moist; their glazed shimmer reflecting the light from the rechargeable lantern which held back the darkness from the dining table. What else had he been forced to endure?

After dinner, I directed him to the room he would be sleeping in, and he went in to shower. I washed the used plates and then returned to the living room, collapsing onto one of the sofas. Jide emerged from the room, holding some clothes.

"I made these," he said, with a note of pride in his voice.

I took the clothes and examined them. The designs were simple but neatly done. His minimalistic approach struck me. "Impressive. You must have been a very good tailor then."

"Maybe," he muttered. There was less confidence in his voice and I wondered again what could have made him abandon something he was so talented at.

He wore a white singlet and boxer shorts. The orange light from the lantern gave his skin a creamy hue and cast a huge shadow behind him. My eyes lingered on his broad chest and prominent muscles for a moment and then with a yawn, I announced that I was going to bed. He thanked me again for letting him spend the night and packed the clothes he'd shown me into a polythene bag.

I entered my bedroom, bolted the door behind me and pressed my ear against the wood, listening to his receding footsteps. I heard the door to his room creak open, then shut; the bed springs groaning under his weight.

As I stood at the foot of my bed, unfurling the mosquito net which hung above, the enormity of what I had done hit me.

I had allowed a strange man into my home.

FOUR

I lay in bed for a long while, just staring at my phone. The sound of gentle knocking at the door made me raise my head. I was uncertain at first, but it came again. *Knock knock.*

"Jide?" I called. "Is that you?"

"Yes."

What did he want? Did he need a wrapper? Did the batteries in the rechargeable lamp run out? Against my better judgment, I pushed my bed clothes aside and got up.

"Do you need something?" I began, leaning against the knob. The door opened a crack.

"Yes," he said, pushing it all the way. "Only you."

His eyes were filled with pure longing. When he cupped my cheek with his hand, I surrendered and let my eyelids close. The kiss was like a forbidden fruit, sweet and tantalizing, yet dangerous and taboo. I could feel our hearts beating in sync, like thunder and lightning in a rainstorm. The next moment, a force jerked me away from him.

The raucous crowing of Mama Tunde's roosters was a timely alarm. I sat up and reached for my phone on the bedside table. 6:54am. I was covered in sweat and my heart was beating like a wild thing trapped in a cage. It took me a minute to realize I was no longer dreaming. It was all both funny and stupid. I had a boyfriend whom I loved, and Jide would be gone before noon.

Outside, in the living room, the subject of my dream was bent over, sweeping. The muscles on his back flexed with each movement. He raised the broom when he saw me.

"Good morning, Ma."

"It's Stella, Jide. Good morning. Hope you slept well?"

"Yes, I did," He said, laying the broom down. "Your nightgown is beautiful. Did you make that?"

His compliment caught me off guard. I stared down at my pink nightgown as if I was seeing it for the first time and just then realized I was not wearing a bra. I threw my arms across my chest, and seeming to sense my discomfort, he returned to his sweeping.

"I don't make nightgowns," I said, turning to hide my embarrassment. I wanted to tell him not to bother with the cleaning, that he need not do any chores as a form of repayment for last night, and that I would be leaving for the shop in an hour. Instead, I found myself as mute as a clock that stopped ticking.

Breakfast was a meal of plantain and eggs. "This is my favourite food," Jide said, between mouthfuls.

Sitting across from his satisfied face, I asked about his plans. "What time would you be leaving?"

His voice became barely audible.

"To be honest, I have nowhere to go. I lied about having a friend because I was desperate last evening. But you've done enough. I will go anytime you want me to."

There were alarm bells as my brain grappled with this new information. He looked lost in thought, poking his fork in and out of a wedge of ripe plantain. I felt a surge of pity for him.

"You can stay here for like a week and figure yourself out."

"You'd do that for me?" He fell to his knees, hands clasped, and with tears in his eyes.

"Sure," I said, standing up to leave.

"Thank you. Thank you so much, Ma."

"Stella. Call me Stella."

It felt good seeing him bask in relief.

FIVE

After a week, it dawned on me that Jide had no plans of leaving. I realized also, that the idea did not trouble me too much. He made himself useful - he was charming, funny and had no bad habits per se. His jokes had me laughing long into the night and became a fitting end to my stressful days.

As the days passed, it became normal to hear his baritone voice humming in the living room as I prepared dinner in the kitchen, so normal that I feared sending him away would upend things and turn the world on its head. On the other hand, I felt mortified by the scandalous nature of the whole arrangement: a young unmarried woman cohabiting with a young man.

"Your brother is handsome," Mama Tunde remarked one morning as she set down the drinking trough in her hand. Her fowls rushed forward and dipped their beaks to drink, clucking and squawking. My own throat itched as I assessed the manifold implications of her harmless comment. Her widened eyes were a warning that a smile would not pass for an answer.

"He is not my brother," I said, finally.

I watched her eyebrows jump as her smile disappeared.

"He is just a friend."

"What of Daniel? Is he aware of this your handsome 'friend?'"

I laughed and patted her shoulder, "Ma, it is not what you think."

But in a way, her reaction was a catalyst. As I walked down to the shop, I tried to find the best way to broach the subject with my boyfriend. I had been putting it off for far too long, and I knew I needed to get things cleared up before a rivulet of concern became a surging stream of trouble.

That afternoon, I set out for Amuwo-Odofin. It was where his family lived. I wanted to tell him everything; especially about the difficulty I was having in sending Jide away. As I neared the house, however, a feeling of dread crawled and nestled in my stomach. Would he take it the wrong way? Would he empathize? If he disagreed, would he be able to help me come up with some other solution? I battled with these, and a thousand other questions until I was in front of the gate.

The famed 'Green Building' was in clear need of some renovation. The once vibrant green paint was now faded and dull, and areas close to the zinc roof were peeling off due to constant contact with water. The red Volvo parked out front, was the only thing adding a splash of color to the surroundings.

Dan welcomed me with open arms and a smile which faded as I got round to the subject that had brought me there. "You mean you have been living with another man under one roof for over a week?"

He shook his head in disbelief.

"Hey," I said, gesturing towards the inner room where his father snored. I did not want his shouting to wake him. "Dan, it is not exactly like that. He was stranded and had nowhere to go…"

"Stranded, my foot! Like, I don't even know you anymore! How could you do this? How could you allow a man to live with you without my consent?"

"Your consent? As my Lord and personal Saviour?"

I looked at him as he paced the sitting room and imagined a faceoff between him and Jide. He was smaller, although tall enough for a twenty-five year old. Jide was older, more muscular, and looked like a schoolyard bully. An open confrontation would not work. I struggled to find words to calm him down. "I would have told him to come and stay with you, but I feared your father would not approve."

He stared at me. "Do you listen to yourself at all? Why don't you simply send him on his way? Are you his mother?"

"If you were stranded like that, is that what you would like?"

He shook his head and walked out, slamming the door behind him. The loud bang roused his father, but the old man was either too tired, or enjoying his sleep a bit too much to be disturbed.

I stood in the middle of the living room, bereft of answers and feeling like a child with a fishbone lodged in her throat. When it was clear Dan wasn't going to see me off, I left for home; more confused than ever. Why was he overreacting? He had always praised my kindness to people, especially to strangers.

What was wrong this time?

SIX

I spent weeks trying to make Dan understand. One Saturday evening, he came by the shop. I looked up in alarm as he rushed in, ignoring the greetings from my apprentices. "I am just coming from the house. You didn't tell me you were housing a full-grown man!" he cried out, his chest rising and falling fast.

Sensing trouble brewing, the girls excused themselves.

"I asked him to leave and he refused, saying that I have no right to drive him away from your house. So, I will make it simple for you. You have to choose between me and that animal, Jide, or whatever he chooses to call himself. It is either he leaves or I leave."

I watched him as he stood in the middle of the shop, shaking in anger. "Sweetheart, I choose you. I will choose you over and over again."

"So, is that fool leaving your house?"

"He is no fool. He is just homeless. And he is not leaving. He has nowhere else to go."

"Oh, wow!" he shouted, moving to stand directly in front of me. "I feared you would say that. I feared you may have lost your mind. Look. I can't take it anymore, Stella. I just can't!"

His words hurt me. Perplexed by my silence, he took a step back. "I am done here. I am done with this confusing relationship. Go ahead and become Mother Teresa. Shelter every lost puppy you find." He stormed out.

I ran after him, calling his name, my tongue finally loose. He never looked back. He stopped a taxi and climbed into the passenger seat. I held the door, begging him to understand and even promised to send Jide away. My pleas didn't move him.

The taxi zoomed off and left me kneeling by the roadside, watching in tears as the only man I had ever loved disappeared into the distance. When I got to my feet, a small crowd had gathered around my shop. They shook their heads in pity as I trudged back, barefoot, my measuring tape around my neck.

My apprentices were at the door of the shop when I returned, extending their sympathies.

"Madam, sorry."

"Aunty, sorry o. He will calm down."

I nodded and dismissed them for the day. Picking up my keys, I locked up and walked away. I didn't want to break down in front of all the neighbours.

Jide was in the kitchen when I returned. The aroma of the jollof rice he was cooking wafted to my nostrils as I sat down on the sofa. He emerged from the kitchen to meet me on the verge of tears.

It was the curious look on his face that opened the floodgates.

"Dan left me!" I wailed. "Dan left me!"

He sat on the arm of the sofa and held my shoulder. I shrank from his touch.

"Your boyfriend," Jide said. "He come by the house. Very angry. I am so sorry if my presence bring problems between you two."

I didn't respond. I couldn't. Seeing the vistas of an amazing future I had planned with Dan going up in smokes still mortified me.

"He will realize his mistake and come back," Jide said. "You are an amazing lady and the dream of every reasonable man."

His words offered little consolation, but they took me by surprise. It felt good to be described in superlative terms. I cried some more before going to bed, refusing his offer of dinner. Delicious as it smelled, I had no appetite. I felt a deep void and couldn't shake the feeling that my world was crumbling.

The beautiful life I had imagined with Dan just turned to sawdust.

SEVEN

It's often said that the first stage after any break-up, is denial. I found out for myself the following day. I had dialed Dan throughout the day, but got the same response—silence. Even then, I held on to the hope that he just wasn't ready to speak to me, or that he was away from his phone.

At about 4pm, just as I waved goodbye to a customer who had come for a fitting, I heard the shrill note of my SMS notification and I hurried into the shop to open the message. The words were short, terse and direct: *Stop calling my line. You made your choice. It's over. Dan.*

I stared at the phone, reading the message again and again. A wave of anger coursed through me. Dan was being stupid, allowing his jealousy to blind him. I took out my fury on my sewing machine, pedaling until my legs ached.

It was dark when I closed the shop. The girls had since gone home. The full moon was out, casting long shadows of folks traversing the busy street.

I boarded a bus headed for Dan's home, squeezing myself in-between two fat market women smelling of fresh fish. The woman on my left tore open a nylon bag with her teeth, squeezing out the dark brown content onto the crumpled loaf of bread on her lap. I squirmed in disgust as she munched away at her sandwich of bread and beans. The bus crawled through the mind-numbing Lagos traffic.

After two hours, I alighted at the bus-stop close to Dan's house and walked through their street to the gate. Wiping my eyes dry of every tear, I knocked. A square hole in the gate slid open and a familiar eye peeped through. The square closed followed by a shuffle of feet. Adamu the gateman emerged.

"Good evening, Aunty Stella," he said in his heavily-accented English. "Oga Dan…" He rubbed his neck.

"Wetin happen?" I asked.

"Oga Dan say make I no allow you to come again."

"Ah. When he talk that one?" I forced a smile, trying to hide my embarrassment.

"This evening. Today, today."

"Okay, tell him that I have come to see him. Tell him it is urgent."

He disappeared into the building, locking the gate behind him. I stood outside like a castaway, the cold breeze forming goose pimples on my arms. I folded them at first, and when that didn't help I rubbed my palms to keep warm.

At the end of the street, some men surrounded a *suya* stand, the charcoal fire giving off an orange glow which illuminated the darkness. I looked away from the light. Why did I want Jide to stay with me at the risk of ruining my relationship with Dan? Was it out of a need to be charitable? Or were my motives more selfish? Jide was handsome, smart and great company, but was there something more? The more I thought about everything, the more confused I grew.

Just as I tried to dial Dan's number one more time, the gate unlocked. Adamu emerged with a sad look on his face. "Oga Dan say him no wan see you."

I felt bile rise in my throat. "Did you tell him that I have been outside here in the cold and darkness, waiting to see him?" I asked.

Adamu nodded, avoiding my gaze. "I tell am."

Fresh tears clouded my eyes. I turned and left, without another word.

I got home by 9.30pm. Jide was watching television, his hairy thighs uncovered by his boxer shorts. I acknowledged his greetings and sat down, exhausted.

"I didn't know you closed this late," he said.

I said nothing, my eyes fixed on the face of the State Governor as he gave a speech, his round eyeglasses perched on the tip of his nose.

"Did Dan call you?" Jide asked.

My anger surged and I jerked upright. "It's none of your business, okay? If you must know, it's over between Dan and I."

My big toe hit a stool as I stormed out of the room, sending a sharp pain down my spine. I slammed the bedroom door behind me, dropped to the floor and sobbed.

Moments later, I heard a soft knock on my bedroom door and opened it to find Jide standing there, his head hung in contrition.

"I am sorry for everything…all the trouble," he said.

"You don't need to apologize," I responded. "I was the one who lashed out at you. I have been under a lot of stress."

He hugged me and then after a small hesitation, kissed my lips. My initial shock morphed to something else, something softer. The kiss felt so good and surreal, setting loose strange sensations, so I held him and kissed him back. It was slow at first but grew intense as our tongues melted into each other. I drew him into the room, emotions building up as his hands made their way around my body, flinging away every item of clothing I had on.

As I laid on the bed, his hand freed my breasts from my bra and his full lips encircled my nipples. A soft moan escaped me as his hands wandered between my thighs and found my core. When he slid his manhood inside me, I felt at one with the universe. His repeated thrusts filled the room with my moans. I couldn't stop moving. I couldn't keep my mouth shut. I held him tight and rode the frenzy to its head, after which we collapsed onto the bed, exhausted. It was like nothing I had experienced before.

With that masterstroke, Jide's hold on me was cemented.

EIGHT

The next morning, everything was different. The plastic flowers in the ceramic vase on my dressing stand were so vibrant, I could have sworn they gave off a sweet fragrance. I snuggled close to Jide, and his eyes flickered open as I stroked his beard.

"Good morning, Ma," he said, smiling.

"Call me 'Ma' one more time!"

"Or what?" He grinned, mischief dancing in his eyes.

He clasped my breasts in his hands and tickled me till I was roaring in laughter as I rolled off the bed.

As I walked across the room, picking my way around the clothes strewn on the floor, I caught my reflection in the mirror, smiling like a fool.

"You are so beautiful," Jide said.

He was naked on the bed, with a light in his eyes.

I picked up his singlet and boxer shorts and threw them at him. "Cover up, please."

"Why?" he laughed as he began to pull on his shorts. "It's not like there are children here."

There will soon be if we keep this up, I thought, biting my lower lip. I had not yet fully examined my reasons for reciprocating his advances. I didn't want to think about Dan, but my mind was made up on what to do next.

"You are coming with me to the shop today," I said as he made to leave the room.

"Really?" he turned to me in surprise. "That will be great."

We got to my second shop, mid-morning. "You own this place too?" He shook his head in disbelief.

"Yes," I smiled. I enjoyed the look on his face but I was also beginning to feel self-conscious.

"How old are you?" he asked.

"You don't ask a woman her age."

He was insistent. "Answer joor!"

"Twenty-one."

"*Chineke Nna!*" he whistled.

True, I was a far cry from the little girl who had come to Lagos for the first time, four years ago— all her earthly possessions fitting into one small Ghana-must-go bag. But I had gone through the fire to be moulded into what I was now.

I finished top of my class in secondary school at sixteen. With my ambition intact and my good command of English, I knew I would fit in wherever I found myself. The plan was simple. Go to Lagos to stay with some relatives and either learn a trade or go to the university - whichever they could afford. The village held no future for me.

Clothes and fashion had always fascinated me from childhood. Once, I had made a skirt from a jute sack using only a needle and thread when I was just ten. Every Sunday, I would sit in church, mouth half-open as I admired women in their flashy outfits as they danced past during the offertory.

So, when my aunt in Apapa asked me what I would like to do in Lagos, my answer was ready. "Tailoring." She sent me off to a fashion designer friend from Church named Madam Ese.

It took me three years to finally stand on my own, and get out from under Madam Ese's wing. Three years of toil, tears and uncertainty. Slowly, the horizon became clear and I figured I had found my ticket out of poverty as my skill blossomed. I knew I was gifted and that if I kept working at the pace I did, creating new designs, it would not be long before word would spread. And spread, it did. At twenty-one, I was doing well by all Lagos standards.

Many of my customers were rich society ladies who needed new clothes which could make them stand out every weekend at owambe parties and events. I created clothes that stood out in their styles and intricacies and these 'Lagos Madams' paid very well. I lived in a well-furnished two-bedroom flat in Egbeda and had two shops with three apprentices working with me.

I allowed Jide to try his hand at sewing that day, using a spare length of cotton material. He made a small shirt that would fit a boy of five, complete with collar and buttons. He was fast, deft and creative. Looking at the work again, it struck me that Jide could be a vital addition. Through him, I could expand into sewing male attires. I gave him a space in my second shop and helped him start off his tailoring. In time, he turned out to be better than he'd claimed.

Dan became my past, and Jide spent many more nights in my bed.

NINE

By the sixth month, Jide had many customers and was doing well. I was very happy to see him flourish, perhaps so happy that I missed the first signs of trouble.

It was Ebele, the apprentice with whom Jide shared my second shop, who first brought it to my notice.

"Aunty, Uncle Jide has been disturbing me o!" she told me one day, at the close of work.

We were alone in the shop. I searched her face for any possible sign of mischief.

"What do you mean?" I asked.

"He has been toasting me. The other day, he hit my bum-bum."

My palms went to my mouth. "*Isi gini?*"

She repeated herself, this time in Igbo, her tone more forceful than before.

"And," she continued, "Some women come to the shop to look for him. He will then take them to the house."

I was enraged. "How long has this been going on?" I asked her, my hands on my head.

"Like some weeks now," she said, looking at the floor.

"And you are just telling me?" I hollered.

She shifted back in fear.

I knew my quarrel was not with her. Chewing on my emotions, I dismissed her and went home.

Jide was not in when I entered the house. I sat on the sofa, wondering how best to confront him. I dozed off in the midst of all the anguish, and was woken around midnight by the slamming of the front door. Jide stood before me, looking ruffled and reeking of alcohol. He murmured greetings and staggered to his room. I waited for some time, and then entered his room to meet him already fast asleep, still fully dressed. I bent over his face and saw something that startled me and confirmed my worst fears– a lipstick stain on the collar of his shirt.

Flicking off the light switch, I dragged myself to my bedroom in tears.

TEN

The next morning, I was up before dawn. My mind wandered, mulling over everything Ebele had told me; piecing together all my findings. If the stories were true, then I was in a big mess. Fortified with my anger and proof, I stormed into his room and roused him from sleep.

"Wake up, you filthy, lying, cheating drunkard!"

He opened his eyes and stared at me. They were bloodshot but I could see that he was surprised by my countenance. Ignoring me, he slid out of the bed and kicked off his shoes.

"Are you cheating on me with other women?" I asked, standing with my arms akimbo.

He continued removing his trousers.

"You are keeping quiet, abi?" I asked, still fuming. "Coming home in the middle of the night, dead drunk with lipstick stains all over your shirt, that is your new style, eh?"

Jide's eyes went to his shirt, his hands trying in vain to hide the telltale faint red smear. His reaction was all the proof I needed to confirm my fears. I grabbed him by his shirt's collar, shaking him and demanding an explanation. His eyes bulged out at me and with one violent motion, he broke free from my grip and pushed me to the ground. A wave of nausea hit me.

"Don't you ever talk to me like that again!" he said.

"You disgust me!" I rose to my feet and rushed to the toilet in time to vomit into the bowl. I retched till tears came to my eyes.

The day was only going to get worse. After the episode that morning, I felt unwell throughout the day. That evening, certain that I was suffering from a bout of malaria aggravated by Jide's misbehaviour, I stopped over at a shop on my street.

Nurse Titi, the owner of the place, was in her fifties and well known in the street because of her numerous children – eight of them, despite the vigorous Family Planning campaign she championed.

"Tailor, you look pale," she said, after we had exchanged pleasantries. "What is the matter?"

"That's why I came," I said, sitting on a stool facing the table across which she sat. "I have been feeling unwell lately. I even vomited this morning. It is probably malaria."

She nodded. "I will take your blood for a quick test."

Nurse Titi was always quick to recommend tests or extra drugs to increase the bill. There was some detoxifier, vitamin or blood tonic she would recommend with an innocent look. Usually, I would be reluctant to accept whatever extra bit she offered, but I was feeling too ill and wrung out to argue.

She tied a thin, transparent rubber tube around my wrist and hit the back of my palm until some veins appeared. After cleaning the area with alcohol-soaked cotton wool, she pierced my skin with a needle and within seconds, the syringe was filled with my blood. She might have her faults, but her skill was undeniable. Mothers who lived on the street always brought their children to her for her 'painless' injections. She removed the syringe and pressed down on the pierced spot with another bit of cotton wool while she untied the tube. I felt blood rush back towards my palms and pressed down on the cotton wool after she let go, to stop the bleeding.

She disappeared into an adjoining room and I looked around the shop to pass the time. It was windowless, the rotating ceiling fan blowing hot air. Different kinds of medications were stocked on the shelf and appeared to be in competition with the beverages placed next to them. Hanging in front was a carton of condoms. I had always wondered why two sane adults would allow a 'rubber' come in-between their enjoyment. I had never used one, my aversion for them heightened by reports from friends who had, and complained about a diminished feeling.

On the wall were posters, with images drawn on them. One had a caption in bold red ink, 'HIV no dey show for face'; another had the image of a woman surrounded by many children with 'Start Family Planning NOW' written beneath. Nurse Titi came to my mind and I chuckled. Her large brood was the opposite of everything she represented. It was like a bus conductor counselling me not to shout, when it was all they do from dusk till dawn.

The door to the adjoining room opened and she came out, holding a sheet of paper. My amusement disappeared when she opened her mouth.

"You have one plus of malaria," she said. "And you are also pregnant." Noting my surprise, she asked me, "When last did you see your period?"

I thought hard and my heart began to race as it occurred to me that I had not had a period in over two months. I avoided her gaze as I paid for the malaria drugs. I accepted everything she recommended without protest. Leaving her shop, my mind was in turmoil.

In the week after the revelation of my pregnancy, I watched Jide, unsure of how and when to break the news to him. As the days passed, my other fears began to worsen. His womanizing took a different turn. It was as though our fight over lipstick stains had unleashed some demons within him. He barely returned home and when he did, he left very early the next morning. We became strangers under one roof.

I felt what we had slipping away, as fast as it had begun.

ELEVEN

One month after our fight, I returned from the shop in the evening and was arranging his pillows when I found a golden bracelet, tucked between the mattress and the wooden frame of the bed. I never wore bracelets and the sight of one – possibly belonging to a strange woman Jide had brought home in my absence – irked me.

Infuriated, I packed up all the clothes hanging in the wardrobe, dumped them into his bags and carried them to the corridor. I collapsed onto the sofa in the living room, and awaited his return. The room was dim and the chair creaked as I vibrated with fury. What have I done to deserve such disrespect in my house? Was it a crime to help someone in need?

Around midnight, I heard Jide unlock the door and sprang up from the sofa, the bracelet in my hand. He had barely noticed my presence before I exploded.

"Who owns this? Eh?"

He glared at me and went into his room without a word. Minutes later, he rushed out, his eyes red with anger.

"Where are my clothes?" he asked.

"They are in your bag, outside," I said, pointing towards the corridor. "You are leaving my house tonight."

He went outside and began to bring his bags into the house. I blocked the door with my frame. He tried to shove me aside and when I held onto one of his bags like a wildcat, he landed a blow to my head. I fell on the floor, dazed by the force of his raised fist. Arms flailing, I grabbed one of his legs. He kicked me many times. I held on, absorbing every blow, tears blinding my vision.

After some time, he stopped kicking and bent over me, a look of horror on his face. I followed his eyes and let out a loud wail.

The lower part of my nightgown was soaked in blood.

TWELVE

We spent the next day at the hospital. The nurses looked at me with pity and threw eye daggers at Jide as he hovered around my bed, shamefaced. I refused to talk to him and cried non-stop. My head pounded and I didn't know if it was due to my nonstop crying or because of the punches he had rained on me.

The doctor, a bald, elderly man, was furious with Jide. "How can you beat your wife to the point that she loses her unborn child?" he asked.

Jide went on his knees, pleading. "I didn't know she was pregnant. I swear to God!"

The doctor shook his head. "Even if she was not pregnant, is it right for you to hit a woman?"

Jide knelt there like a chastised school boy, looking penitent. After some time, he turned to me. "My love, why didn't you tell me, eh?"

I suppressed the urge to spit at him. "Were you ever at home?"

He fell silent, fear etched on his face.

The doctor touched my swollen face and then held my hand. I felt a fresh surge of tears run down my cheeks. "How are you feeling?" he asked.

"I feel cramps in my lower abdomen. And pains all around my body," I said, shifting to my side.

"You had an incomplete miscarriage. The ultrasound scan we did earlier dated the pregnancy to be around eleven weeks. The cramps are from your womb trying to push out the remaining parts of the dead baby. We will take you to the theatre for an evacuation and give you some drugs to take care of the pains. You will be fine."

In the days that followed our return from the hospital, Jide apologized several times. I ignored him. The thought that he could turn to bite the hands of his benefactor was galling.

To spurn someone who has shown you nothing but kindness was every shade of cruel.

THIRTEEN

It took two months before I forgave him and I did so only with the intervention of Mama Tunde, our caretaker's wife. The elderly woman went to great lengths to prove to me that Jide was a changed man.

The incident had shaken him, she told me, demonstrating how Jide had rolled on the floor of her apartment, refusing to get up until she agreed to intervene in the matter. She ensured that we hugged and kissed before she left, a sign she took to mean that her mission was accomplished.

The following week, Jide came home, whistling, something I had not heard him do in a long while. I was in the kitchen, the pestle rising and falling as I pounded some pieces of cooked yam. On entering the kitchen, he opened the pot and let out a happy shout at the sight of the steaming nsala soup with assorted fish and meat. Bending, he hugged me and kissed my cheeks. I looked at him, wondering what had come over him.

"Pounded yam and nsala soup. Perfect for the occasion," he said, smiling.

"What occasion?" I asked, still trying to figure out why he was acting like a child let loose in a toy store.

We were back on speaking terms, but I was still reticent.

"Baby, I would like to meet with your parents."

I dropped the pestle, wiped the sweat off my brow with the edge of my wrapper and searched his face for signs that he was drunk. He was lucid and his voice sounded serious. In the nine months during which we had lived together, he had never mentioned seeing my parents.

"Why?" I asked, still surprised.

"Because, I want to marry you."

He held my hands and drew me up to my feet. Indeed, he was sober. But this, all this, seemed strange.

"Really?" I asked, still trying to find my voice.

He nodded and hugged me. "You are my angel."

I was awash with emotions, struggling to stop the tears already welling up in my eyes. Maybe, just maybe, there was still hope for us.

We made love that night. Soft and sensual, and then rough, hard and loud, our moans and grunts ferrying the frustrations of the past months over an abyss of nothingness. We landed on the shore of peace, in each other's arms.

The world was fine again - fences mended, broken trust forgiven and every need, fully met.

FOURTEEN

The next weekend, I took Jide to meet with some of my relatives at Apapa. My younger sister, Nkechi, was living with them and attended her make-up classes from their house. The building was in a busy part of the town, just along the expressway, and they lived on the first floor. From the balcony, I saw countless yellow danfo buses with loud, screaming conductors careen down the expressway. The bustle usually continued into the night.

After we had greeted my relatives, Nkechi called me aside. "Stella, who is that guy?" she asked, her hands on her waist.

"He is my boyfriend o!" I said, smiling. My smile disappeared as I read some concern on her face. "What?"

"I don't like him," she said. "He looks too flashy."

"Ha!" I laughed. "Of course, he has to look flashy. He is a tailor. He sews and wears clothes."

Nkechi left me on the balcony, shaking her head as she went inside. I was baffled by her stance. In the living room, Jide was regaling my uncle and his wife with one of his Aba tales; he soon had them reeling with laughter. They seemed to like him and my sister's concerns faded from my mind.

The following week, we travelled to my village, Umueshi, at Jide's request. We boarded the first bus from Iyana-Ipaja going to Owerri which left the park at 6.30am.

The journey was long, a painful reminder of the distance between me and my people. We crossed the Niger Bridge and entered Onitsha around 2pm, our bus taking a short route that led us into Owerri road. It took us two hours to get to Owerri from Onitsha, our journey delayed by the numerous police checkpoints. We disembarked and entered another bus going to Anara, stopping halfway into the journey at Okwelle. Then, we boarded a motorcycle to take us to Umueshi, a distance of about forty-five minutes.

The swaying palm trees, the dusty roads and the windy surroundings were a sharp contrast to the hot, stuffy atmosphere of Lagos. As we made our way into my village, a palm wine tapper shouted his greetings. He was anchored to the tree by a strong girdle made from raffia palm leaves.

The air smelled of decaying mangoes that littered the road, with parts eaten by bats. Further down the road, there were decaying paw-paw fruits with yellow bodies turned brown due to neglect. Some children trailed our motorcycle from the Eke marketplace, their dusty bodies moving as fast as their shrill voices, screaming their welcome.

Mama emerged from the kitchen when she heard the sound of the motorcycle. The children who were chasing us soon reached the compound, about seven of them, panting. Jide gave each of them a crisp twenty naira note and they ran off, ecstatic.

"Stella *nwa m*," Mama said, embracing me. "How are you?"

"I am fine, Mama."

She greeted Jide, then winked at me and led us into the sitting room.

Mama's skin shone. There must be some merits in the black palm kernel oil that she swore by, as the answer to a supple and healthy skin. I made a mental note to ask for some of the oil, to take back to Lagos with me. She stooped a little as she walked, and half of her hair had turned grey. A feeling of sadness crept over me at the realization that the years were catching up with her. She opened the wooden window shutters of the living room to let in fresh air. Calling out to one of my cousins, she instructed him to inform my father, who was at the farm, that he had visitors.

The room seemed smaller to me than it used to be, even though everything was mostly unchanged; Papa's bicycle still rested at one end, close to the wooden cupboard that held all manner of items including kolanuts, alligator pepper and locally-brewed gin. The seats were threadbare, the once-covered foam peeking out at the edges of the worn material. My parents' wedding picture hung on the wall, its black and white quality now rusty-brown with age. The German floor was the same except for the crevices that had widened with time.

Papa entered the room, his hoe slung over his shoulder. His white singlet had some holes. Most of his hair had also gone white, but he stood straight and had some springs in his steps. We stood up to greet him and he smiled.

"Papa!" I screamed, hugging him. I had really missed him.

"Stella *nwa m*," he said. "You look good. *Nnoo nu.*"

He embraced Jide and reached into his old cupboard to fetch some kolanuts and alligator pepper.

After we had eaten kolanuts, Jide presented him with a gallon of palm wine and explained the purpose of his visit. My father immediately sent for two of my uncles and some elders from my kindred, who lived nearby.

When they gathered, Papa asked Jide to repeat what he had said earlier. Jide informed them of his intention to marry me and promised to return later with his people. The men were silent while he spoke. When he was done, Nze Chibogwu, a gaunt old man and the eldest in our clan, cleared his throat. Adjusting his red cap, he spoke in his quavering voice.

"Our people believe that just one person cannot come on a marriage visit." He paused and looked around, attracting nods from the other elders.

"We will tell you what we think when you return with your people."

The next day, we left for Jide's hometown on his insistence that I must meet his people. His town, Umuchu, was in the neighbouring Anambra state, a short distance from Uga, the town at the border of the two states. It took us an hour and half to get to his family house.

The Onuwas lived in a modest bungalow, plastered but not painted. The wall bore circles and numbers, from the house-to-house numbering done during the National census of 1996, and the corrugated sheets on the roof were new.

His mother, an elderly woman with a slight limp, welcomed me with a big hug. She smelled like soap and coconut oil, and I surprised myself by holding the embrace, reluctant to let her go. "I have been asking to meet you," she said, beaming. "Jide told me how helpful you have been to him in Lagos."

I laughed. "Mama, he has also told me many wonderful things about you."

"Where is Emeka?" Jide asked.

Emeka, Jide's younger brother and the older of his two siblings, was the bread-winner of the family. He was a businessman in Onitsha, specializing in tearing down used Japanese cars and selling off their parts. The last child, Chioma, had just finished her secondary school education.

"Emeka went to Onitsha early this morning with your sister. He plans to enroll her for JAMB lessons near his house, so she will be close to him and he can keep an eye on her. You know that girl is a handful. I'm getting too old to be chasing her up and down, and I don't have the heart to even discipline her."

She smiled at me. "Emeka really wanted to see you both, but Chioma's lessons resume tomorrow. Did you notice that he has replaced the old, leaking zinc?"

Jide nodded, turning to take another look at the roof.

Inside the house, after we had eaten, his mother turned to face Jide. "When are we going to pay her dowry?" she asked.

Jide laughed. "Very soon, Mama."

I joined in the laughter as Jide's mum told me stories about his antics as a child. I felt very welcome and loved.

That night, I overheard her asking Jide to promise her that he would marry no other woman but me. I cradled the pillow, smiling as I returned to my sleep.

We headed back to Lagos the next day.

FIFTEEN

In the six years that followed, Jide never made any mention of marriage again. My people waited and waited for him to show up, their patience stretched to borrowed limits. I ran out of excuses to make on his behalf. It felt awkward to bring up the topic and each time, he evaded the subject, slippery as a bar of soap.

What made matters worse was that our neighbours thought that we were married. They called me his 'Madam'. But it was something else, a ghost from the buried past, that would drive me to tears.

I was sweeping his room one morning, moments after he had left the house, when I found a weft of artificial hair near his bed. My heart sank as I raised the mattress and after a thorough search, assembled all the newly discovered evidence: three dissimilar earrings, and a lipstick-stained pillowcase.

I hauled them to Mama Tunde's flat and sat in her living room making my case. I was in tears when I finished. The woman drew me to her bosom, allowing me to sob. She told me in confidence that she had seen Jide on two occasions with different girls at the house when I was not around, but she did not suspect anything since they wore scarves over their heads like 'church people'.

That evening, Jide came home fuming. "What did you tell Mama Tunde?"

"Why are you doing this to me? Eh, Jide? Why are you treating me this way?" I asked.

He sneered and entered his room, muttering something about "showing me pepper since I have refused to mind my business."

The next evening, I returned from the shop and was about to enter my room when I heard some noises coming from the kitchen. I opened the kitchen door to see a young lady, staring at me.

"Who are you? And what are you doing in my kitchen?"

She hissed and eyed me, her insolence palpable. "Who are you?"

Her question infuriated me. I twined my fingers in her hair and dragged her out of the kitchen, flinging her onto one of the sofas in the living room. "You came into my house to ask me questions, abi?"

She sat there, looking stupefied, her initial defiance gone. "Jide brought me here," she said, at the brink of tears.

Her tears left me unmoved. I had no sympathy for a woman who chose to make herself at home in a house where it was obvious another woman already lived. I dragged her up and pushed her towards the door.

"Next time, eh, tell him to take you to a hotel or wherever you prostitutes roam!"

I slammed the door after her, rushed into my room and sank onto the bed, heartbroken. I could not hold back the tears.

I was woken that night by a high-pitched female voice screaming obscenities. I rubbed my eyes, surprised I had fallen asleep. My pillow was damp with tears and my head was pounding, so I was sure I was not dreaming, and yet I was confused when I peered at the clock on my bedroom wall and saw it was past midnight. How could I be hearing a woman's voice in my house at such a time? I scrambled to my feet.

Tiptoeing, I went in the direction of the sound: Jide's room. I opened the door to behold Jide on top of the girl I had tossed out earlier that evening, their naked bodies contorted in passion. They carried on, oblivious of my presence.

I left as I had come, retiring to my bedroom in tears and plugging my ears with my fingers in a bid to block out their moans.

It became a norm, as Jide brought home a different girl each week. There were the fat ones, sometimes three times my size, some with fake-eyelashes and cheap weave-ons. Then, there were slim ones, with their prominent collar bones looking like they had been starved all their lives.

I felt trapped. I made several plans of throwing him out but didn't follow through with them. Pretending that he wasn't there and burying myself in work seemed easier than dislodging an Iroko tree with deep roots. I suffered in silence, wishing that one of the girls would come to some harm during their intense romps and he would be whisked away for manslaughter.

I needed a calamity of such proportions to set me free.

SIXTEEN

After five months, I found out that I was pregnant again. I received the news with mixed feelings. For the most part, I berated myself for getting pregnant for a hopeless man like Jide. Yet, I was grateful for the gift of life growing within me. It was a replacement, I told myself. God was replacing what I lost, and giving me some joy in a life filled with only unhappiness and neglect.

A lot of questions coursed through my mind. It was clear that my child would be born out of wedlock. Will I be able to cope with the stigma? From Jide's actions, I knew I would raise this child alone. How will I manage? I searched my mind for answers and tried to process the situation. In the end, I embraced my circumstances and sought out the nearest hospital to register for antenatal care.

The Antenatal Clinic was like an open market. Almost every day, pregnant women occupied all the benches in the open hall, their bellies at various stages of protrusion. Most had unfazed looks and discussed among themselves, ignoring the elderly nurse seated at the table calling out numbers, her voice hoarse from repeated shouting. A few people, like me, looked frustrated by it all: the newness of the experience, and the stuffy, crowded atmosphere made worse by the noise of ceaseless chatter and occasional laughter.

After we arrived, they asked us to drop our urine and blood samples with the laboratory for basic investigations. I was directed to a room for an ultrasound scan.

I stared at the screen, confused by the black and white images while a man in a white ward coat moved an instrument over my abdomen. He did not bother to explain anything to me and I was too timid to ask.

I returned to the waiting room, handed the lab and scan reports to the nurse and went back to my seat. Was pregnancy worth it? The stress was enormous: monthly and sometimes weekly antenatal visits, the daily intake of the routine drugs, and the burden of carrying an extra weight for a greater part of nine months. For an act we did with men, it seems an unfair punishment to women.

"So wrong."

A woman who looked like she was carrying twins glanced in my direction. She must have heard me. I hissed at the glaring injustice and then closed my eyes to get away from it all, to preserve what was left of my sanity.

A strong nudge on my side woke me. "No be you be number thirty-five?" the woman beside me asked. "Dem don dey call you since."

I rose to my feet. The room was half-empty now and the nurse pointed towards the doctor's office, rolling her eyes at me to register her displeasure.

I entered the air-conditioned room and a middle-aged male doctor greeted me while pointing me to a seat.

"Madam," the doctor began. "Your ultrasound scan showed your baby is doing well."

"Thank God," I said, relieved.

He stared at a pink-coloured slip in his hand. I recognized it as the laboratory investigation result of my blood test and my concern rose as he shook his head. Was something wrong?

"Madam…I'm afraid you also tested positive for HIV 1 and 2."

"What?" I asked in a low voice, as time seemed to stand still.

"I said you tested positive…."

"I heard you, Doctor! But… how come?" I asked, confused, my mind whirling. "I have been faithful to my partner of seven years now, and last year when I did this same test, it was negative!"

"Has your man been faithful to you?" he asked, adjusting his spectacles.

I sank further into the seat, cold to the bone. The next minute, I was in tears.

"Jide has killed me," I cried, my hands on my head.

"Who is Jide?" the doctor asked.

I was too heartbroken to respond.

The doctor shook his head again as he reached across the table and patted my hand. "Whoever he is, just advise him to get tested, okay? The world has not ended, Stella. You have to think of yourself and your baby now."

I nodded, wiping away tears with my left hand as I thanked him.

I came out of his office, trying very hard to stay composed. I felt the eyes of everyone on me, like they knew I had HIV. Leaving the hospital complex, I caught my reflection in one of the glass doors and burst into fresh tears.

My world as I knew it, just collapsed.

SEVENTEEN

It was a miracle that I got home that day, unhurt. I had walked along the road like someone in a trance, disconnected from the blaring car horns and the insults from bus drivers who felt I had a death wish. My legs moved of their own accord, my mind wandering everywhere and nowhere.

People said terrible things about HIV/AIDS. It killed faster than a bullet, had no cure and was one of the deadliest diseases in town. Most of these stories, I had gleaned from bits of gossip by my more talkative customers, some of whom prided themselves as teachers on everything sex.

One of these was Mama Iyabo, a voluptuous woman in her late-thirties, known for her amorous escapades. She had a loud voice, booming laughter and a deep disdain for young girls; especially those below twenty-five, whom she called 'fine, small devils' and blamed as the cause of her broken marriage. We all knew it was her notorious trysts, with both married and unmarried men, that made her husband leave.

"HIV is terrible!" she said, snapping her fingers at the thought of the ailment. She had come to collect her clothes, but as usual, spent hours talking nonstop. "Na so the sickness dry *ore mi* Ese like *bonga* fish. It is terrible!"

The way she described Ese left us horrified. We knew Ese to be a chubby madam. And we knew *bonga* fish.

I pictured myself as the next topic of discussion and cringed at the thought of my name dancing from one set of loose lips to another. If this illness did not kill me, then shame would.

I walked past my shop and straight to my compound. My legs ached as I climbed the stairs, partly due to the trekking and partly due to my broken spirit. As I fumbled for the keys to my flat in my handbag, my hand struck a container. I brought it out and sighed. I had forgotten about it, the bottle of antiretroviral medications given to me to prevent the virus from infecting my baby. It had the word 'Combivir' written in bold. I felt sick as I pushed the bottle back into my bag, dismayed at my new reality - condemned to a lifetime of pills.

Jide was in the living room when I entered, watching television. I sat opposite him, the memories of the past seven years flooding in, without warning, coming with bitter tears.

"Why are you crying?" he asked after a few minutes, interrupting my whimpers.

"The doctor said I have HIV," I blurted out.

"What?" He had a big scowl on his face, which morphed to fear as he realised I was serious. "How? Where did you get it from? Have you been seeing other men?"

I sat up, stung by his words. "What do you mean? Haven't you been the one carrying different women up and down?"

He stared at me, disbelief and confusion written across his face. I felt a wave of disgust as I stared at him, standing there in a pair of boxers, the bulge in his loins housing his tool of destruction. What possessed me to let this devil in? I stormed out of the room.

That night, when I went to inform him that dinner was ready, he was seated on the bed, lost in thought. When I repeated my statement that his meal was ready, he faced the wall, murmuring something about how the bad news I brought home made his appetite disappear.

I shrugged, too tired to argue or even care about how he felt. I had my own thoughts destroying me.

"I was started on medications today. The doctor said you should come and get tested."

"I am not going anywhere."

"Suit yourself," I said, closing the door behind me.

It took two weeks of constant reminders to get him to change his mind. I kept at it because I felt he did not deserve the peace of mind he was looking for by avoiding the truth. Finally worn down, he followed me to the hospital and as I expected, he tested positive too. I checked his face for emotions when the doctor broke the news to him. He showed none. His CD4 count came out to be three hundred. He was started on antiretroviral medications.

There were long stretches of silence when we got home that day, interrupted only by Jide's occasional grunts. He wore a sad face, and ate his dinner without saying a word, as though not talking about our predicament would make it disappear. I took my drugs immediately after dinner and waited for him to do the same. He left the table still sulking, the bottle of drugs clasped in his palm.

Some weeks later as I was cleaning his room, I saw the same bottle of medications in his drawer. Its white seal was unbroken.

I brought it up that evening over dinner. "Why are you not taking your meds?"

He looked at me, shook his head and continued eating.

"You want to die, abi? Have you forgotten that the doctor said HIV only kills when one refuses to take his or her meds? Eh?"

He left the dining table without saying a word.

EIGHTEEN

As time passed, my world gradually came back into focus. There was a lot to prepare for, especially as my expected date of delivery approached.

I was at the shop one evening talking to Mama Chiboy, one of my customers, when the pains struck.

"Are you alright?" she asked, a look of concern on her face. She had penetrating eyes that made one feel uneasy whenever she stared.

I held my waist and nodded. "It's just this waist pain I have been having since yesterday."

Her eyes widened in alarm. "It may be labour o!"

I raised my hands in protest. "But my due date is still four days away."

"Labour can come before or after the expected date of delivery na," she insisted.

I made to stand when I felt a gush of wetness from between my thighs and down my legs.

Mama Chiboy stared at the wet patch on my dress and nodded. "Your water don break."

Her voice bore a tone of certainty, the sort that came with multiple personal experiences.

Ebele rushed to my side and with Mama Chiboy's help, got me into a taxi. I made sure to carry the delivery bag. The nurses had drummed it into our ears in the weekly antenatal visits. It contained necessities required for admission once labour began. I had brought it to the shop with me every day, just as the nurse told us, as my due date drew near. I groaned throughout the journey to the General Hospital, each new wave of pain more troubling than the last.

The nurse at the prenatal ward stole glances at me, shifting her gaze to my folder whenever our eyes met. I had grown accustomed to such looks during my antenatal visits, especially from nurses. The discovery of my HIV status usually had some strange effect on them, an effect so powerful that I could see it in their eyes. You deserve it. You were the one that refused to close your legs.

I was admitted into the ward, a small, poorly-lit room with six beds. Three of the beds were occupied, the patients sitting up, with their big tummies resting between their thighs. One of them, a young lady, was shouting.

The midwife pointed me to the empty bed closest to the wall and walked up to the bed of the shouting woman. "Na me give you belle? Eh? Why are you disturbing the whole of Lagos now?"

"E dey pain me," the lady said, in tears.

"Ooooh! When you dey do am, when e dey sweet you, you no sabi say e go later pain you? Abeg, keep quiet!"

Her comments drew laughter from some nurses in the room as well as the other two pregnant women. Another nurse threw in a consoling remark: that the pain would get less with subsequent pregnancies.

Another wave of contractions struck. My waist was on fire. The midwife, on hearing my agony, approached my bedside, rolling the blue-coloured bed screen along. She surrounded my bed with the screen and as she pulled on a second pair of latex gloves on her already gloved hands, I saw that look.

"Is your husband aware of your status?" she asked.

I shook my head. "I am not married. But my partner is aware."

She shrugged. "I am Matron Bisi. Open your legs, let me check you."

I laid back on the bed, raised my loose gown and parted my thighs, my legs flexed at the knees. Placing her left hand on my abdomen, she inserted the index and middle fingers of her other hand in between my thighs. I felt the fingers within me, ascending with some difficulty. Then I felt the fingers move apart, separating till I winced in pain.

She brought them out, the fingers covered in bloody mucus. "Six cm," she said, smiling. The number meant nothing to me, but her smile was reassuring. "You are making progress."

After removing the first set of gloves, she placed a brown, small, funnel-shaped plastic on my lower abdomen. She bent her head, her right ear on the smaller end of the plastic funnel, and held up her wristwatch as she listened, her lips moving.

"Your baby's heartbeat is fine," she said, raising her head. "You should deliver before midnight, if everything goes according to plan."

I nodded and thanked her.

Ebele appeared at the door, carrying the bag containing my delivery items.

"Where is Jide?" I asked, looking at the door.

She sighed. "I met him in his shop and gave him the news. He just nodded and continued sewing."

Her eyes darted across the room as she drew close a plastic seat beside the bed. I unzipped the bag to ensure all the items were there: pads, olive oil, delivery mat, plastic cord clamp, toilet rolls, wrappers, baby clothes.

Ebele hissed. "This thing Uncle Jide is doing to you is not good. You bought all this with your money and just to be present, just to show face, he cannot."

I closed the bag. "Some men are like that. They will act deaf and dumb during your pregnancy as if your protruding abdomen was an everyday occurrence. Still act deaf and dumb to everything else, including running the home and raising the children. They are the type you should avoid."

Just then, Nkechi, my sister, rushed into the ward, sweating. "I was in the market when I got your text message. If you see the kain race I pick, eh!"

I forced a smile, a sense of relief sweeping through me as she grabbed my hand in hers.

The pain increased with each passing hour. The other crying lady was taken to the labour ward and soon after, news filtered in that she had been delivered of a baby girl.

"Na wa o!" Nurse Bisi said, clapping her hands. "Na so so girl, girl we dey born today for this hospital. Some days e go be boy, boy. Hmmm!"

I walked around the prenatal ward, restless, unable to control the strong urge to bear down. I had felt a strong urge to defecate earlier but my straining at the white bowl yielded nothing.

"Na the baby head wey dey press down dey make you feel that way," Matron Bisi said, noting my frustration as I took my seat on the bed covered with a red mackintosh sheet. "Your Oga still never come?"

I shook my head and continued breathing through my mouth as she had instructed me to do earlier.

"My shift don end. I will hand over to the night shift nurse. You go born well, you hear?" I nodded but, in my heart, I wished she would stay longer.

The night shift nurse was tall and dark, with a serious face. She approached my bed with Nurse Bisi.

"Wait outside," she said, shifting her gaze from Nkechi to Ebele. They stood up and left the ward.

"I was told your case is unique," she began. "We will try to minimize the contact your baby has with your blood to reduce the risk of transmission. Also, we will commence the baby on some antiretroviral drugs after birth, to prevent transmission. Have you been taking your medications?"

I nodded, surprised at the hurdles my unborn child would need to jump to win the war against this virus. "Can I breastfeed my baby? The doctor said it can be transmitted through breast milk."

"Yes, there is a twenty percent risk of transmission through breast milk. But since you have been taking your meds all through pregnancy, your viral load should be very low. This reduces to a minimum the risk of transmission during breastfeeding or the delivery process itself. So, you can breastfeed your baby for three months and stop or you can use infant formula. It depends on your pocket."

"You just cleared my confusion. Thank you. I would love to breastfeed my baby."

"Born the baby first nau," Matron Bisi said, dragging the evening nurse to another patient's bedside.

They took me to the labour room some minutes before midnight. The pain had become excruciating and I had the persistent feeling of a mass inching downwards between my legs. The contractions were more frequent and forceful. I groaned as I waited for the next wave of severe pain - my waist being cut into two with a blunt cutlass.

Half an hour of pain later, with one last push, I was delivered of a baby girl; her pink, beautiful form revealed after all the blood on her had been cleaned off. She smelled of olive oil and her skin shone. Holding her in my arms and assuaging her tiny, crying frame, I felt a surge of hope within. I drew her closer to me till her ear was level with my mouth and I whispered a name that had been on my mind all along, a name that summed up all that she represented.

Victory.

NINETEEN

I stared at the ceiling fan whirling in the postnatal ward, trying to take my mind off the dull ache between my legs. Victory lay in the cot beside me, asleep. I had put her to breast some hours after delivery but noted with frustration that my breast had refused to produce any milk. Her large, innocent eyes looked up at me as I removed the nipple from her mouth. I forced a smile and laid her in the bedside cot, praying that she would sleep without making any fuss.

"Drink this," Nkechi said, handing me a bowl of pepper soup. "The nurse said that it will help your breast milk to flow."

I collected the steaming bowl and placed it on the bedside cupboard. "What will my baby eat?"

I drew the cot close and sat up. The baby slept in peace, oblivious of my worries.

"Try and get some sleep," Nkechi said. "You have been through a lot."

Victory stirred in her sleep, moved her right thumb into her mouth and started sucking it. I watched her tiny, pink lips move, producing a soft, clucking sound.

"The nurse said she will give her glucose water in the morning. It will give her strength before your breast milk starts flowing. Just eat, then go to sleep," Nkechi said. I felt tears prickle my eyes, wondering how I would have coped without my sister.

I let her fuss over me and took some of the pepper soup. I was nodding off when she spread a wrapper on the floor and laid down.

We were discharged after two days. As we left the hospital, we bade goodbye to the nurses and patients who had become like family. Nurse Bisi saw us off to the hospital gate.

She held my shoulders, "You are a strong woman. Your daughter will bring you joy."

Her words brought tears to my eyes. We both knew exactly how strong I needed to be, considering my unique circumstances. "Amen. Thank you so much."

We stopped an empty taxi and boarded it. I sat in the back with Nkechi, while Ebele climbed into the passenger seat. The driver, an old man with a missing front tooth, offered his congratulations.

"Madam, well done o. E easy to get belle, but e no easy to born."

The ride home was silent save for occasional curses from the taxi driver, aimed at errant motorists or pedestrians. I struggled to keep awake, adjusting the shawl covering Victory as she slept in my arms. On the ride my mind drifted to Jide. Other ladies are fortunate to meet their Prince Charming or Knight in shining armour. Me? I was gifted an *agbaya*, an overgrown baby, who did not even care to be present at the birth of his own child. How unfair can life get?

He was not at home when we returned. Nkechi and Ebele helped me assemble the cot I had bought in preparation and I placed Victory inside it after she had been fed. My breast milk had finally begun to flow one full day after my baby's arrival, much to my relief.

I laid on the bed, exhausted. The dull pain was spreading to my thighs from the site where one of the Matrons had given me a 'generous cut' so that Victory's head could emerge, a common occurrence associated with first time births. I felt the tip of the suture poke my skin each time I walked. The Matron assured me it would be absorbed by my body over time, and encouraged me to have 'Sitz-Baths' – sitting in a basin of warm water that had a sprinkling of salt.

"I should 'just sit'?"

"Yes," she had said. "Just sit. It will facilitate the healing of your cut."

Victory stirred and began to cry. I unfastened my bra and put her to breast.

I heard the door to my room open later that night. Jide was standing there, looking at the cot, his face taut. I turned to face the wall.

"Welcome back," he said. "Sorry, I couldn't come."

"You couldn't? For two days?"

He approached the cot and reached out to touch the baby.

"Did you wash your hands?"

He withdrew his hands and stared at the baby as she slept. "She looks like me."

"It is too early to tell."

"She has my nose. And look at her ears, she will be dark eventually."

"She was started on antiretroviral meds. Syrups. The nurses said that she would be fine. "

I was answering the questions I felt he ought to be asking.

He sat on one end of the bed, saying nothing.

"You have a child now, Jide. Some things will have to change. Have you started taking your meds?"

He got up and, without a word, left the room.

My milk flowed so much that it kept soaking the front of my clothes. Funny how I had prayed for milk and was now exasperated by the jets of warm liquid that had me changing bras several times a day. Victory suckled to her fill. She fed every hour, even at night. The sheer work of keeping awake, changing diapers, bathing the baby and suckling her left me drained. I was groggy during the day and almost went mad from sleep deprivation. Nkechi was on hand to help and Ebele ensured my shops were open and we delivered on the orders we had received.

Some of our neighbours came to see the baby. Mama Tunde came visiting with her children, bringing a cockerel and some yam tubers. Some of my more regular customers came too, most dropping cash gifts and baby items before they left.

Their visits touched me. I did not see myself as popular and loved by many, but the support I received filled me with gratitude - a deep feeling that rose like water, bathing me with fresh emotions. I made a list of everyone that visited with a mental note to strengthen the bond we shared, in the future.

Their goodwill gave me strength.

TWENTY

The day I saw the rashes, Jide had entered my room, bare bodied, wearing just a pair of boxer shorts. Victory was four months old, propped up in her cot, babbling. When he bent to carry her, there were multiple dark spots spread over his back. Some were also on his abdomen, covered in parts by his body hair.

"How long have you had these rashes?" I asked.

He looked surprised and studied them in the mirror. "They are scars from the chicken-pox I had as a child."

"Chicken-pox, Jide? How come I haven't noticed them since?"

One closer look, the rashes were larger than chicken pox scars and looked fresh, not healed. "You will need to see a doctor."

"I am not going anywhere." He slammed the door as he left, startling Victory who broke into tears.

I carried her and rocked her to sleep.

In one month, it became evident that Jide had lost weight. His well-fitted trousers were loose on him and his shorts appeared too large for his frame. He also had a stubborn wet cough that defied all medications.

Ebele called me aside one morning at the shop. "Something is wrong with Uncle Jide. He runs out every hour to go to the toilet and he don lean finish."

I asked Ebele to look after Victory and went to my second shop, where I found Jide alone, sewing. I sat on one of the stools and watched him as he sewed for fifteen minutes, undisturbed by my presence.

"You're losing weight."

He continued sewing, his gaze on the fabric. "I know."

"We are going to the hospital. Now."

"Let me finish this piece. The customer is coming to collect it today."

About half an hour later, we made our way to the hospital on foot. The hospital was on the next street, the first floor of a white two-storey building. A folder was opened for him at the reception. After waiting for an hour, it was our turn to see the doctor.

The doctor was a young man who spoke fluent English. He asked some questions and examined Jide. He shook his head as he looked at the rashes and then filled out forms for laboratory tests for us.

Some of the test results were ready in an hour. The doctor called us into his office. "Your husband's HIV has progressed to AIDS," he said, his eyes moving from me to Jide.

Doctor, this man is not my husband. He brought this on himself.

The doctor's voice stopped my thoughts. "He can still recover if he is placed on intravenous medications. We will admit him and commence the antiretrovirals immediately."

Jide was quiet as the doctor spoke, like a man in the dock listening to his sentencing.

We thanked the doctor and followed a nurse who led us to the ward. It was a room with four beds. There was one other patient in the room, a young boy with a cast on his leg. We were assigned the bed closest to the door. I settled Jide into it and then left to bring our things and leave instructions for my workers.

Jide spent two weeks at the hospital. He made significant progress; the coughing subsided and the diarrhoea stopped. I went home every morning and evening to bathe Victory and cuddle her for a while. Nkechi learnt how to mix baby formula, and helped feed her whenever I was away.

Jide was placed on antiretroviral meds and warned by the doctor to comply with taking them before he was discharged.

He returned to the house a changed man, his face radiant and his mien, calm. He smiled more often and was quick to tell everyone how God delivered him from untimely death. He also played more with Victory as he realized that HIV was not spread through body contact.

The change was not to last.

TWENTY-ONE

One evening, I returned to find him jumping and screaming. I set down Victory on the sofa. "What happened?" I asked, trying to make sense of his jubilation.

"I have been healed of my HIV," he said.

Prancing about the room, he broke into a dance and ended with a church chorus. He went to the table and grabbed the bottle containing his medications.

I couldn't make sense of his theatrics. "What are you doing?"

"I don't need this anymore," he said, running out of the room.

I followed him. He was headed to the toilet and before I could utter a word, he emptied the tablets into the toilet bowl and flushed. He raised both hands, fists clenched. "I am free!"

His maniacal display worried me. "Why not do a blood test before you conclude?"

"God healed me and you are talking of a test?" He shut his door in my face and resumed singing.

I went into my room, still shaken by what I had just witnessed. Victory was silent, her eyes looking into my face. I stopped at the mirror to straighten my hair and barely recognized who I saw.

A tired, weary girl in her late-twenties yoked to a stubborn and unfaithful madman.

TWENTY-TWO

Children grow fast. Victory walked at ten months and by the time she turned one, she could communicate her basic needs to me. She was a strong girl, had not fallen sick and kept herself busy at the shop by picking pieces of materials and playing with them. I made matching gowns for her and her ragdoll. It was her favorite toy and best friend. She spoke to it often, especially after a scolding.

I had two new apprentices. Ebele had finished her training but decided to stay on in the shop. She helped me out with taking care of Victory and I paid her a salary, with a commission on any work she did.

I left Jide alone to run the second shop and build his clientele of male customers.

One afternoon, a young boy who lived in the area ran in, drenched. The rain was heavy outside. The wind and thunder chased each other, drowning out the noise of sewing machines inside my shop.

"Oyibo, what is it?" I asked, as the boy made his way to where I sat working.

"Aunty Stella," he replied, at the top of his voice, "It is Uncle Jide o! He just fell down in his shop."

I sprang up and ran out into the rain, in the direction of my second shop.

"Madam, thank God you don come," Oyibo's mother said, as soon as she saw me. She too was soaking wet.

"Wetin happen?" I asked, confused. Jide was lying on the floor, barely conscious but breathing.

"Na like this we see am for ground. E never even reach five minutes, so I send Oyibo to call you come."

I flagged a cab and with her help, carried Jide inside the car and headed for the hospital.

We were referred to the General Hospital, another forty-five minutes' drive from the first hospital we went to.

"Are you his wife?" the doctor asked me, after Jide had been admitted into the ward.

"His girlfriend," I said, looking away.

"Are you aware of his condition?" he continued. I could sense the dilemma in his voice.

"Yes. We both have HIV but he has refused to take his meds for some time now."

"Why? How long?" There was a look of concern on his face.

"One year," I replied.

The doctor shook his head and started writing inside Jide's folder.

After he was placed on intravenous medications, I watched Jide as he slept. Was I surprised that he collapsed? Not at all. It was obvious where he was headed when he refused to take his tablets. It was just a matter of time before the other shoe dropped.

Play stupid games, win stupid prizes.

TWENTY-THREE

I was outside the ward when I saw Ebele and Victory approach. My little girl ran towards me, her school bag hanging on her back.

"V-Darling!" I cried as I lifted her up and carried her in my arms. She gave a happy smile, exposing her incomplete dentition.

"How is Oga Jide?" Ebele asked.

I sighed. "He is on admission. He has opened his eyes."

"Thank God. I have to get back to the shop. Let me know if you need anything."

I nodded and carried Victory into the ward. She seemed oblivious of her environment until she saw her dad. "Daddy!" she called out, reaching down from my arms to touch him.

"Shhhh! He is sleeping," I said in a low voice, setting her down beside the bed.

The ward was a small room with four beds. Two nurses were on duty. One of the nurses was going from bed to bed, administering injections and handing out tablets. The other sat at a table at one end of the room, writing in a book.

"Ma-Ma, see." Victory was raising her dog-eared notebook, which she had opened to a page. A shapeless object was drawn in red crayon and coloured in pink, blue and black.

"You drew that?"

She nodded.

"It's beautiful." I said, kissing her forehead. Lifting her up, we went outside the ward to bathe our faces in the evening breeze.

After two days, Jide, who had now become fully conscious, was responding to questions by nodding or shaking his head. He was also beginning to recognize visitors.

"Your immune system was severely compromised and so the disease progressed to affect several organs." the doctor said after he had examined him. Jide stared at him, showing no emotions.

"Doctor, I warned him o!" I turned to face Jide. "Why on earth will you stop taking your meds?"

The doctor cleared his throat. "The good news is that the rampaging virus may still be overcome if you start taking your meds daily, without fail."

Jide's eyes lit up. "I will get well?"

The doctor nodded. "It is possible. But only if you keep taking your meds."

As Jide assured the doctor that he will take his medications, I chuckled at my lack of faith in his new earnestness. I had heard these stories and fervent promises before. It didn't end well.

Early the next morning, while the sky was still dark, Jide's younger brother, Emeka, came to the hospital. I had called to inform him as soon as Jide was hospitalized. He looked exhausted, having travelled all night from Onitsha.

Emerging from the doctor's office, he came to Jide's bedside and stared at his brother.

"I am taking him to the East, closer to home," he said. "I spoke with my siblings and Mama."

"Don't you think he should stay here for some time before travelling such a long distance?"

He shook his head. "I have a doctor friend with whom I have made some arrangements. Also, the more he stays here, the more bills he accumulates."

There was no need to protest further as Emeka seemed to have his mind made up. I shrugged and opened the flask of food I brought for Jide.

"Try and eat," I urged him. "It is your favourite."

Jide ate only three spoons of the eggs and plantains and stopped. I covered the flask and gave him a bottle of water to drink. The nurse arrived with his medication, which he swallowed.

"Please, I would love you to come with us, Stella," Emeka said.

"To the East?" The last thing on my mind was to travel.

"You can return as soon as we get him admitted into my friend's hospital."

A short trip. Not more than a couple of days. To the East and back. "When do you plan to leave?"

He looked at this watch. "This morning, say before 11am, whenever you are ready."

"But you just arrived, Emeka. Why not rest for one day, at least?" I asked.

Emeka shook his head. "I feel strong enough, and I have so much to do back home. I can't afford to spend an extra day in Lagos."

Jide's eyes were on me. "Please, Stella."

I gave in. "Alright then. Let me make arrangements for my daughter and instruct my apprentices."

I left the hospital and went to beg my sister Nkechi to stay at my place for the time I would be away. She was to keep an eye on the girls at the shop.

"How long are you staying?" she asked.

"About two or three days. I will come back as soon as they admit him into the hospital."

On my way back, I stopped by Victory's daycare to see her. She was excited to see me, and my heart ached that I would be leaving her for some days. Since she was born, we've not spent a night apart.

"Mummy will be gone for some days. But Aunty Nkechi will bathe you, feed you and take you to school, you hear?"

She nodded, but I knew she did not understand. There is no way to explain a mother's absence. The void is felt and the pain is borne till she surfaces.

We left the hospital around 11.30am with a frail Jide. At the motor park, we saw a bus, nearly filled with passengers. A tout paced around the vehicle, waving a bandana in the air as he shouted, "Onitsha! Onitsha!" There were three seats left.

Shortly after Emeka paid our fares, the bus was on its way.

TWENTY-FOUR

We got to Onitsha around 7pm. A group of boys rushed towards the bus as it entered the park, offering to carry the baggage of passengers with their wheelbarrows for a small fee.

Jide was shaking when we alighted. He had vomited twice during the journey and I had to clean him up with the spare wrapper I had. He had also refused to take any food, for fear that it would worsen his diarrhoea, so I knew he was running on empty.

Emeka's wife, Uloma, was waiting for us at the park. "*Nwanyi Oma*," she greeted me, smiling. "You have tried so much."

I hugged her in response.

She led us outside the park to a waiting Toyota Corolla. Emeka drove, navigating the street roads out to the express. I pressed my nose to the window, enjoying the draft of fresh air from the open front windows. The last thing I saw before my eyelids shut in exhaustion were the iron beams of the Niger Bridge.

I was awoken by a light flashing on my face. Shielding my face, I let my eyes adjust and realized we were at a police check-point. The green luminescence on my watch beamed. 9:08pm.

"Where are we?" I asked, when the car started moving again.

"Delta State," Emeka said. "My friend's hospital is in Udu, very close to Warri."

We drove for another hour before the car slowed down and turned into a gate. It pulled up inside a large compound housing the hospital. Emeka parked close to the main entrance and honked several times. A nurse ran out, spoke with Emeka and then went inside. She returned with a wheelchair with which we moved Jide into the Emergency room.

A young doctor came to meet us. "Your brother?" he asked Emeka, pointing at Jide.

"Yes," Emeka said.

The doctor asked a series of questions, all the while writing in a folder. When he was done, a young lady came from the lab to collect Jide's blood for some tests.

"We will admit him," he said, closing the folder. "If all goes well, your brother will recover fully."

We were taken to the ward. After Jide had been given a bed, Emeka and his wife left, promising to return in the morning. He handed me ten thousand naira just as they were leaving.

"For food and drugs," he said.

TWENTY-FIVE

After two weeks, Jide was strong enough to walk around the ward, unaided. He joked about his 'husband material' being "minus hundred". The statement often drew laughter from other patients in the ward.

He got better by the day. Once, he asked me for a pen and paper. He was strong enough to write and draw caricatures. There were no radios or TVs so this was his only form of entertainment. I even heard the doctor talk to the nurses about discharging him.

Emeka and his wife visited only twice, each time leaving with the promise to come the next day, only to surface after a week. This attitude riled me. But what worried me most, was my unplanned, prolonged absence and the effect it was having on Victory. Despite Nkechi's assurances, I feared that she was not eating right or sleeping well. My anxiety grew every day, made worse by daily reminders of the grim reality at the hospital.

The ward was in a separate building- a yellow bungalow with mosquito nets on its windows, adjacent to the main ward. Its paint was being washed off by the rains but the ceiling boards were intact. All the patients in the ward looked very ill. There were five beds in all. Jide was Bed one. The last was vacant. Bed two was a pretty, young woman being looked after by her mother and sister. Her boyfriend visited every day.

One afternoon, I met him sobbing at the entrance of the ward.

"What happened?" I asked.

"Why are people so wicked?" He was sobbing. "Can you believe that Lilian knew she had HIV and never mentioned it to me? She allowed me to make love to her unprotected for two years."

"You mean she has been aware for two years?"

"She said so herself," he said, heading in the direction of the lab.

I stood there in the corridor, bewildered. Fifteen minutes later, he ran towards me with a broad smile. "I tested negative!" He stopped to catch his breath. "I pray that I test negative again in three months."

That was the last time I saw him at the hospital. And who could blame him?

Bed three was a blind man probably in his fifties. He was admitted a week after we arrived. He was being looked after by his newly married wife.

One morning, she was shouting at the doctor, during the ward rounds by his bedside. "How can he have HIV when he cannot see? I am telling you that this is all spiritual," she said.

The doctor tried to hush her as her voice could be heard by others over the barrier around his bed.

She continued to protest. "I have been tested and I am negative. How do you reconcile that?"

As the doctor walked away, she continued, "His children confessed to striking him with blindness and I know they are responsible for this."

Bed four was another young woman, nursed by her fiancé - my first time seeing a man nurse a sick person. She had been in the ward for only four days. He was always there, cleaning, washing and bringing her food. I was impressed.

One evening, I brought out some dirty clothes to wash and met her sitting outside the ward. Her fiancé had gone out to buy food.

"You have such a nice, supportive man," I said.

She responded with a stare. "Do you know anything about HIV?"

"Oh," I avoided her eyes. "Well, I know it is not a death sentence."

She let out a loud hiss, and then scoffed, "That's very easy for you to say."

"Look. I also have HIV, okay?" I said. "It is not a big deal. Just take your drugs daily and you will be fine."

The expression on her face softened. "I like your confidence."

I washed for a while in silence. She watched the grass around the building. I followed her eyes to see what had caught her interest. It was a blue butterfly moving from one blade of grass to another.

"He caused all this." There was anger in her voice.

"How?" I asked, confused. "Is he positive too?"

"No. He is negative. And he is the only man I have known."

Her last statement deepened my growing confusion. "So how come he caused it?"

"I got pregnant for him last year." She wiped off a tear from the corner of her left eye. "We had been dating for six years. When I told him I was pregnant, he said he was not ready and that we could not start a family yet. He had just started his business then, and was struggling to find his feet. He suggested that I abort the baby."

I pushed aside the bucket containing the clothes I was rinsing, wiped my hands dry with my wrapper and sat down beside her.

"He took me to this place. There were like twenty young girls sitting in a room. We paid near the entrance and I was given a number and shown where to sit. Every now and then, a young girl would come out. A voice behind the door would call out 'Next!' and the next girl in line would enter. When it was my turn, my first instinct was to run. Lying in a bowl were bloody metallic instruments, adjacent to a tattered couch. One old man with blood-stained gloves motioned me to lie on the couch. I did and he told me to spread my legs."

She was fighting back the tears at this point. "When he was done, I could barely walk out of the room. Yet, the pain I felt from my lower abdomen was nothing compared to the anguish I felt in my heart. I felt betrayed, hopeless and useless."

I held her shoulders.

"I did not speak to him for a week," she continued. "When I eventually did, he could not withstand the venom I poured on him. He shed tears like a flogged child." Her body was quivering, surging with emotions the memories have unleashed. "His business eventually took off. He came to see my people for the initial marriage rites. We were attending marriage classes in my church. Last week, the church requested we run some basic tests – blood group, genotype and viral screening. My HIV test came out positive."

I didn't know how to respond. "Whatever we cannot change, we have to embrace and try to overcome. No matter how dark the night, morning eventually comes."

When she had wiped her tears, we talked about other things. Her fiancé returned with the food.

"I am not hungry," she said with a smile. He looked at us, unsure what to do and then entered the ward.

When I finished washing, she helped me spread the clothes. We watched the sun go down basking in the ambience of the orange sky.

"Tomorrow, we will rise with the sun, stronger than ever before," I said.

TWENTY-SIX

"Oh God!" I muttered under my breath. The offensive smell was distinct. Turning my nose away, I rose up to do what had become a routine in the past five days: cleaning watery shit. For the fifth time that morning, Jide had soiled himself. It baffled me how one could make rapid recovery within three weeks and fall apart in the six days following it. He had refused to eat anything and as a result, lost the little flesh that was trying to form on his miserable frame.

As I undid the rope girding his trousers, I looked at him. He was the shadow of a man, a bag of bones held together by thin, mottled, dark skin. Every muscle in his body seemed to have withered away along with his strength and vigour. His eyes were sunken, lying deep in their sockets and each time they swung in my direction, they spoke of so much misery. His cheek bones jutted out, competing for attention with a protruding jaw bone. His chest was reduced to a display of prominent ribs ending in a cliff, below which his depressed abdomen lay like an excavated river basin. His thighs were now mere shrivelled skin wrapped over long bones.

I put on a pair of milky-white latex gloves and raised my head above the blue screen which shielded us from the rest of the ward. Some of the patients and their caregivers cast sympathetic glances in my direction. A door squeaked as two people left the ward, unable to stand the smell coming from our corner.

I bent Jide over and pulled down his trousers, his dark, shrunken penis resting atop a tuft of discoloured pubic hair. Pale brown, watery faeces stained his inner thighs and formed a dark patch at the rear of his trousers. The bed was spared only by an impervious sheet of mackintosh.

I set to work, cleaning him up with a towel that I dipped in soapy, disinfected water. After I had wiped away every trace of faeces, I turned him on his side, to clean the bed. When I was done, I covered him from the waist down in a dark blue wrapper and removed the gloves which had turned brown. Jide's eyes were fixed on me as he opened his mouth to say something. His tongue was coated with a thick white film that had resisted intense brushing.

"What is it?" I asked.

He sighed and closed his mouth. Whatever he intended to say was swallowed with difficulty along with spittle.

"Jide, why are you refusing food and meds, eh? Do you want to die?" I asked.

He turned his face to the wall. I felt the gel of silence between us hardening into indifference.

That week was hell. Jide's health took a left turn, and raced downhill. He refused both food and medications. The pleas of the doctor and nurses went unheeded. He was placed on intravenous fluids. But he kept pulling out the cannula through which the fluids were administered.

After the ward rounds that morning, the doctor explained to me that he was left with no choice but to refer him to another hospital. I pleaded for more time to make some arrangements with his family. The hospital agreed that we could leave the next day.

He didn't make it to the morning.

TWENTY-SEVEN

Jide died exactly five minutes to midnight. We were meant to leave the hospital for Delta State Teaching Hospital, Oghara, and now his ashen body lay lifeless and rigid on the bed.

The nurses came to cover the body. They removed the urinary catheter, and the cannula in his right hand. I watched them for a few minutes, feeling numb, and then I walked away, heading outside the ward, a folded sheet of paper in my hand.

Earlier that evening, I had discovered that he was breathing with difficulty and propped him up. He motioned to me, pointing to his shirt's breast pocket. I retrieved a folded sheet of paper from it.

"Please read it," he said, amidst gasps.

I ran to call the nurse. When we returned, he was no longer breathing.

I left the ward to clear my head. I sat on the pavement outside, the surrounding darkness keeping me company. Some crickets chirped in the nearby bush, oblivious of the hurricane of emotions within me. I waited for the tears to come. As I gazed into the lonely night sky, devoid of stars, I wondered what Jide's death meant for me. I had become numb to the pain he had caused, so numb that I could not feel anger for all he had done. Rather, I felt pity. Pity, guilt, contempt and shame for bringing him upon myself. The shame weighed more than the guilt and contempt put together. The weight of those emotions soaked up all my tears, leaving me with none to shed.

Still numb, I called Emeka and informed him of what had happened. I heard him heave a sigh and hang up after expressing his condolences. I put my phone's torchlight on, and unfolded the sheet of paper that was still clenched in my palm. A letter. I knew Jide wrote and drew a lot some weeks back when he made good recovery but he didn't show me this. His bad grammar was unmistakable.

Stella m,

Me, am a broken man. I was broken eight years ago when I stand in front of your shop to beg for place to stay the night. You try to repair me. You try well well. Asa nwa, you loved much. I never deserve it, that kind of love. I never know love in my life apart from when I was a small child before I run from home.

Since then, na abuse, problem and bad things. I see bad thing. I did bad things also. Oga Aboy my master at Aba, sex me by force, many times. Every day, I was feeling pains. I told nobody. When I could not stand it again, I ran away one early morning and enter bus to take me far, far to Lagos. That is same evening I see you.

You show me love. But it was too much. I wanted to run from past things. I followed woman thinking their moaning stop my pains. But pain stronger than woman. I expecting you push me away out of your house and out of your life. But you hang there, you did not push me away. I remember that day you miscarriage. I drunk too much and beat you because of nonsense. I still feel that guilty till today.

I don't mention marriage with you because I know I will be bad husband and bad father. I still trying to understanding my life and we have another baby? I can't manage. It is surprising when I see you wanting it, to marry. I don't want you to feel disappoint, so I stay in silence.

When I saw my HIV positive, I know everything has end. I deserve it by my bad things I do. It surprise me that I become

*fine after I start the drugs. Nobody knows I am HIV. Is not fair.
I suppose to be punish. I suppose to have the sickness and to suffer.*

*This is when I stop the drugs. I tell you I am healed. I want
to become very sick so that you be tired and you will go. But you
don't go. You stay and believe I will be well.*

*I watch you clean my shit. I see you clean my vomit. I watch
you take care of my one baby, Victory. I know she will be strong
and lovely woman, like her Mama. Take care of her well. I know
she will not remember my face when she grow up. Give her warning
to stay far away from men who do like me. Our problems is plenty
and we scatter everything in the end.*

*I give you an example. After I write this letter, I will stop
taking food and drug. You will think I try to kill myself. But I
am try to make you free. For eight years, you are bird in cage.
When I go, you will fly free.*

*Also, I am tired of this my nonsense body. I will go the other
side. I know I can still stay here. But I am a broken man. I am
not a saint. So, maybe no angel Michael or Gabriel. I don't know
what I will see. I fear to think about it.*

*I have not tell you this in eight years. I love you, too much.
But it don't matter now because when you are reading this letter,
I am dead.*

Sorry.

His letter took me to a mountain and left me
teetering at the edge.

TWENTY-EIGHT

Out of the depths I cry to You, O Lord. Lord, hear my voice. The silence in the empty church contrasted with the turbulence in my heart. Staring at the crucifix, tears streaming down my cheeks, I could not find words to express the storm within. Only David's plea from the one hundred and thirtieth Psalm did justice to my anguish.

I returned to Lagos three days back, a mess. The events of the previous month shook me to the foundations of my being. Since I returned, I had spent most of my time alone, trying to make sense of it all. I had helped a random person - a nice, commendable thing to do. Yet, that singular act of kindness was the birth of evil. And to think that there is a God up there who allowed it all to happen. I let out a howl and broke down again. The crucifix was a symbol of injustice and I was seething with anger.

As I stormed out of the church, I checked the time. 9:17pm.

I decided to walk home. Victory was in the care of my younger sister as I sought to get a handle on myself. I had lost interest in everything, including life itself. Two voices argued in my head.

"There is no reason to go on living. Kill yourself. Put yourself out of this pain. End it now," one voice said.

"Don't mind her," the other voice said. "Jide was your past. Victory is your future. If you kill yourself, you will make life miserable for Victory."

"Why fight a lost cause? Your case is hopeless."

"Only a moron goes down without a fight." On and on they went.

The road was busy. Conductors were swinging from the doors of the yellow buses that whizzed past, reeling off their destinations like a song. I ran across to the other side of the road. My run was ill-timed and was greeted with the blaring of horns and screeching of tyres.

The irate drivers hurled expletives. "Witch! You wan die?"

I paid little attention. Maybe I did want the buses to run over me and crush my problems beneath their tires. I wasn't sure. I just continued walking. Passing a roundabout, I made a turn into the next street.

The street was dark and quiet, the night silence punctuated by the hum of generators in the surrounding homes. There were still a few open stalls. I lived at the end of the adjacent street. As I walked down, I realized I could make out the figures of about five people gathering next to a large LAWMA dumpster. They were conversing. One of them carried a flashlight, which he directed at a box lying on the ground. I was about to pass them when I heard a child's wail.

The man with the flashlight, probably in his mid-twenties, pointed at the carton again. I followed the light. Inside the carton, wrapped in a piece of cloth, was a baby. Teary-eyed, the baby let out another high-pitched cry. The part of the cloth covering the lower half was soaking wet.

"Wetin happen? Wey the Mama?" I asked, touching the woman.

She shrank from my touch, eyes narrowed with that suspicion that lives in every Lagosian; fed daily by tales of abduction and missing body parts. When she got a better look at me, she relaxed.

"We no know o!" she began. "I just dey close my kiosk when Olanrewaju run come meet me say him see one pikin around the refuse dump."

"E be like say na the mama leave am for here," said the fellow with the flashlight. "Na me first hear the cry, naim I go call Mama Sulia. A bouncing baby boy. Some people can be very heartless." He shook his head, turned and walked away. The other men soon dispersed.

I was left with Mama Sulia and the crying baby. "We need to take this child to the Police Station. This baby cannot stay here all night," I said, looking at her.

"Police kè?" she asked, clapping her hands. "Abeg, I no want Police wahala o!" She started moving away.

"Please Madam, since your house is close, take in the baby for the night. Maybe the mother will come for her baby in the morning."

Mama Sulia glared at me from head to toe. "You want my husband to kill me, abi? Me, I get eight children. Eight! And we dey stay for one room." With that, she hurried off in the direction of her kiosk. I stood in the gathering darkness, staring down at the baby.

A gust of cold wind swept past me bringing with it a crude sense of loneliness. I bent down and took a closer look. The baby was quiet, as if aware of his predicament. I proceeded to unwrap the wet cloth around him, noticing his body felt too warm. As I touched him, he began to cry.

"Shhhhh!" I tried to quieten him down. "Your mother will soon come."

Placing the carton under my left arm, I went into the adjacent compound.

The compound had a bungalow with many rooms. I knocked on the first door. A stern-looking woman answered.

"*Kilode?* Who you be? Eh? Why you dey disturb person by this time of the night?"

"Madam no vex." I said, searching for the right words. "I saw this pikin beside the refuse dump and I wan know if you sabi the mother."

"Hmmm," the woman said, eyeing the carton with suspicion.

In an instant, her tone changed. "*Olosh!* I resemble mumu for your eye, abi? Gerrrout!" she said, slamming the door in my face. I stood there, stunned.

"Kafayat, who be that?" a man asked her, his voice coming to me from behind the closed door.

"Na one mad woman wey carry one pikin dey waka about..."

I left the compound in a hurry. Me, a mad woman? That accusation could metamorphose into kidnapper or thief and with no witnesses to support my story, things could get dangerous for me.

I went straight to my compound and knocked at the caretaker's flat. His son, Tunde, answered the door.

"I didn't know you were back," Mama Tunde said, as she emerged from the room. She looked at the carton after I sat down.

"I came back three days ago," I said, forcing a smile. "Jide is dead." I stopped short of bursting into tears.

"*O ma se o! Pele.*" She hugged me. "*Aani riru e mo,*" she added, snapping her fingers. "No more deaths."

"Amen," I said, relaxing on the sofa.

"Who get pikin?" She pointed to the carton.

"I found this baby near the refuse dump at the end of Olaitan Street, abandoned in the cold. Which kain mother would do that?" I brought out the baby from the carton.

The child started crying. He was light-skinned with jet-black curly hair. His umbilical stump was still attached, tied at the end with a dirty thread. He could not have been more than a week old. His body was warm as I handed him over to Mama Tunde.

"Tunde, bring clean wrapper come," she called out. "And check the First Aid box for liquid Paracetamol," she added.

Tunde returned with the items. We cleaned up the baby and gave him the Paracetamol syrup.

Mama Tunde handed the baby over to me. "We go carry am go police station in the morning. Clean the navel with methylated spirit and cotton wool. And feed the baby."

"Thank you, Ma," I said, rising to leave. "Goodnight."

I was worn-out when I got to my flat. I prepared some milk for the baby and he gulped it down, clutching my finger with his small palm. After he was fed and slept off on the bed, I set up Victory's old cot and laid him inside it.

I changed into my pink pyjamas, but was too tired to button it.

TWENTY-NINE

The quiet of the night was shattered by the sirens of police cars. I rushed to the window to understand what was going on, and saw half a dozen armed officers climbing up the stairs. The knock on the door roused Nkechi and Victory from sleep. My heart pounded as I approached the door.

"Open. Police!" a voice shouted from the other side.

I rubbed my palms to rid them of sweat. Was it the baby? How did they get here so fast? Couldn't they wait till morning? My mind raced with possible scenarios, each one more frightening than the last. Nkechi and Victory were now wide awake, standing on either side of me. I took a deep breath and opened the door to face the officers.

"Madam, we have received reports of an abducted baby," one of the officers said. "We need to search your apartment for any signs of the child."

Abducted? I didn't abduct him! I tried to tell them this was all a mistake, but no sound came out. Why was this happening? I stepped aside to let the officers in. They searched the apartment several times, but found nothing.

After what felt like hours, they finally excused themselves, leaving Nkechi, Victory, and I alone. I tried to go back to sleep but couldn't.

Where did the baby go?

THIRTY

I woke up with a start, my pyjamas soaked with sweat. The nightmares had been frequent since Jide's demise. But last night was different. Despite all my suicidal thoughts, somewhere in my subconscious, I had willed a life to be saved and helped the baby to escape police capture.

He squirmed in the cot, breaking into a cry. I picked him up and rocked him, cooing under my breath till his fussing stopped. I prepared a fresh bottle of milk, fed him, bathed him and then dressed him up in Victory's old clothes. Done, I laid him back in the cot, where he gurgled to himself and drifted off to sleep again.

I was taking my bath when I heard a knock on my door. "Coming!" I shouted, toweling off and throwing on a loose gown. When I finally answered the door, it was Mama Tunde.

"*E kaaro*, Ma," I greeted, as she entered the living room.

"*Kaaro*, my daughter," she replied, smiling. "I hope the baby gree you sleep?"

"Yes," I said, leading her to my room. She leaned over the cot and ran her fingers through his soft hair.

"He slept throughout the night," I said. "Maybe because I fed him well."

An hour later, we arrived at the police station. A burly constable was at the front desk.

"Yes?" he queried, smoothening his unruly moustache. "Women, what can I do for you?"

"I found this baby near a refuse dump at Olaitan Street last night," I began. "No one could say who dropped him there. So we decided to bring him here and report the matter."

The policeman looked confused. "Jubril!" he called out to another policeman behind a wooden counter. "Come and hear this story." He was shaking his head, staring at us as his colleague walked over.

"Wetin happen?" Jubril asked.

I narrated the previous night's events.

"Haba!" Jubril exclaimed, turning to the other policeman. "Amodu, e fit be one mad woman born am, come forget am for the refuse dump. Or e fit still be all these small, small girls weydey carry belle anyhow. Una go write statement for us."

He left and returned with a sheet of paper and a pen. I handed the baby over to Mama Tunde and penned down a statement of how I had found the baby, trying to be as accurate as possible.

"We don write statement finish, where we go drop the baby?" Mama Tunde asked Officer Amodu, as I handed him the finished statement. The policeman let out a hearty laugh.

"Drop the baby, kè?" he asked, still laughing. "Go and look at the signpost outside. It says Police Station, not orphanage." Noticing the shock on our faces, he stopped laughing.

"Look, women, what you did was commendable. Heroic, even. But we don't have the facility to nurse week-old babies."

He pointed towards the window. "There used to be an orphanage down the street but it was closed down last month."

"Why?" I asked.

He shook his head. "The owners turned it into a baby factory. They would gather teenage girls, get them pregnant, and nurse them within the walls for nine months until delivery. After delivery, they sell the children to willing couples or individuals. Male children were going for as high as seven hundred thousand naira while the females were being sold for five hundred thousand each." He paused for dramatic effect, as though he enjoyed seeing the shock on our faces. "The mothers were given between fifty to hundred thousand naira depending on the sex of the baby and their negotiating power. I heard they were paid more if the baby was male."

The other policeman concurred, adding further details on how the baby factory business was outed by concerned citizens, as Mama Tunde and I listened. After some more fruitless conversation, we left the Police Station with the baby. The policemen told us the best they could do was to contact us whenever they got news of a missing child matching the description and circumstances surrounding that of the baby I found.

As we walked past the closed orphanage, my mind replayed the stories the policemen had told us. I could picture the faces of those teenage girls, passing through the excruciating pains of labour, and get handed 'peanuts' afterwards, their babies - gone. It was cruelty in its most inhumane form, fuelled by poverty.

I had seen those walls and the gate to the orphanage before. But I never knew what went on behind them.

We entered a bus to Ketu and located another Motherless' Babies home which Mama Tunde had remembered. The Proprietor appeared touched by our story. "I would have taken him in but for two problems," she said. "One, we have exceeded our capacity. Add that to the fact that funding is becoming difficult. Second, our youngest child is five years old. It will be difficult to raise a newborn here. You can bring him back in three years' time."

I stormed out of her office, disappointed, but sure of what my next move would be. Such an innocent child deserved better than to be rejected thrice in the space of a few hours. First by his mother, then the police, and now a Motherless Babies' home. All the while, the baby slept in my arms, with no care in the world, as though he trusted every move I would make on his behalf.

When we boarded another bus on the way home, the irony of the situation struck me. All the bus passengers were solicitous of the bundle in my arms, offering the usual greetings given to new mothers. To them, I had just given birth and Mama Tunde was my mother.

"Mummy baby, well done o."

"Cover his head a little, make breeze no blow that soft part. Ehen, like that."

"Such a fine boy. Yellow paw-paw."

"Driver, no dey enter pothole na! There's a baby here. Small, small."

Their kind words surrounded us as the bus moved along, but it stirred in me a deep sadness. While their love was genuine, it wasn't enough. If I handed the baby to anyone in the bus at that moment, they would reject him too and it wouldn't be their fault. Sometimes, life was just hard for no reason.

The good news was that unlike them, I could do something about a newborn found in a carton laying in darkness. Just the day before, I was struggling, fishing for reasons to stay alive. Now, I have one.

"Wetin you go do now?" Mama Tunde asked me in a low voice, staring at the baby in my arms.

"I will keep the baby for now," I replied, smiling down at the bundle in my arms.

Till the mother shows up.

THIRTY-ONE

Two weeks passed. The mother did not show up. I had settled into my new role of nursing a newborn, bathing him, feeding him and changing his diapers. Victory could not get enough of the new baby. I introduced him to her as 'her little brother'.

"Baby! Baby!" she would scream in her tiny voice. "Where is my teddy?"

It was a new rhyme she learnt at daycare. She ended the song by touching him in the cot.

The day Victory asked me the baby's name, it struck me that I had not yet named the baby. After some thinking, I settled for Uchechukwu, meaning 'the will of God'. The name spoke of the child's story and its intersection with mine - an affirmation of belief, a statement of submission and a call to surrender to one's fate.

The next Friday, we were at the church for his baptism. Nkechi had volunteered to be his godmother. He was christened Francis.

"Stella."

I was sure I heard someone call my name. I was at the hospital to collect my antiretrovirals and give Uche his six weeks oral polio immunization.

"Stella." The voice was familiar. When I turned, my handbag fell from my hand.

Standing before me was Dan, my ex-boyfriend, grinning. "Dan!" I looked at him as though he were an apparition and touched his arm to be sure. He looked different. Clad in a white ward coat, with a stethoscope around his neck, his name tag read 'Dr. Daniel Olisa'.

"What are you doing in our hospital?" he asked, still smiling.

"You work here?"

He nodded.

"I came to collect some medications."

I kept stealing glances at him as he walked me down the hallway.

"How come?" I pointed at his outfit. "The last time I saw you..."

"Stella, it has been eight years," he said, breaking into an awkward laugh. "Many things have changed."

He stopped, looked at me and shifted his gaze to the baby strapped to my back. I didn't look away.

"I can see you have a new baby." He touched Uche's cheeks.

"Yes."

He tried to force a smile but I saw beneath the facade. He was a simple man, so simple that his eyes always betrayed him.

Looking into his eyes at that instant, I saw pain.

THIRTY-TWO

"Mummy, your phone!" Victory entered the kitchen, handing me the ringing handset. I smiled as I pressed it next to my ear.

"How is your day going?" Dan asked. He sounded tired.

"Great, though stressful," I replied. "Just closed from the shop and trying to prepare food for the kids. How was work?"

"Work was good. I just returned from the hospital. I was planning to come over this evening, say by 7pm."

"OK. How is Madam?" I asked. "You can bring her along."

"She is currently not in town but I will extend your regards."

Over the last one year, Dan and I had rekindled our friendship since the day we met at the hospital. We exchanged contacts and he came to see me after work. There was so much to catch up on. He told me about being devastated by our break-up and having to battle with low self-esteem for some time, since, in his own words, 'his fellow man snatched his woman from him'. Out of frustration, he had picked a JAMB form and chose to study Medicine.

"Why Medicine?" I asked.

"There were many reasons. But mainly because I figured six years would be long enough to forget you," he said, smiling. "I channelled all my anger and frustration into study and it bore fruit. Sometimes, a break-up is a wake-up call."

Not for me, I mumbled. I was happy for him. He told me about his girlfriend whom he was planning to marry and I was glad that he found happiness again.

I put off the gas cooker and set the pot down. The jollof rice was done.

"Vicky!" I called out. She ran into the kitchen, puffing both cheeks, her hair standing up in points.

"Get me some plantains."

She dashed off in an energetic blur. Victory was approaching three years old and was turning into a sweet, hyperactive girl. She brought me two unripe plantains and I smiled again.

"These green ones are not yet ripe. Yellow ones are the ripe ones. We fry only the yellow ripe ones," I said, pointing to the ripe plantains lying separately beside the fridge. She returned with four ripe plantains.

"Is your brother still sleeping?" I asked.

She nodded.

When we finished frying the plantains, I brought out the transparent flask containing Uche's sterilized feeding bottles and prepared his formula. The doorbell rang and I checked my watch. 6.55pm.

I went to answer the door.

"Unkuyu Dan!" Victory screamed, hugging him as he entered.

Just then, the lights went off. "Why did you take our light?" I asked Dan in feigned annoyance as I groped in the darkness for my rechargeable lantern. It was charging beside the television stand. I switched it on, lifted the curtains and opened the louvres of the windows to let in fresh air.

"Omo, this country, eh," Dan said, mopping up sweat from his brow.

"When will we start having constant electricity?" He sat on the sofa facing the television.

"Constant? Do you know how much I spend on fuelling the generator at my shop? One thousand naira daily. That amounts to close to thirty thousand naira monthly. Only on fueling generator!"

Uche decided to remind us all of his existence by giving off a loud wail and I ran to the bedroom to fetch him. He reached up to me from his cot, wet-eyed and irritable. The blackout and the noise from nearby generators had woken him. I picked his feeding bottle from the kitchen and joined Dan and Victory in the living room. Dan was showing her some pictures of animals on his phone.

"Mummy, why did they take light?" Victory asked, turning to me as I fed Uche. I thought for a moment.

"Maybe one of the workers just got bored of giving us too much," I said, smiling. Dan reeled in laughter.

Just then, as though on cue, the lights came back on. "Up NEPA!" Victory and I shouted. I handed over the baby to Dan, then switched on the ceiling fan, closed the windows and brought down the curtains.

"It is no longer NEPA," he said. "It's not been NEPA for a long, long time."

"They can bear any name they like. Let them just give us light," I said, switching off the rechargeable lantern.

"What have you been feeding this boy?" Dan asked, holding the baby up.

Uche giggled.

"Milk o! Just infant formula," I replied, beaming. "The pikin sabi chop. Na for him head all my tailor money dey go."

I left for the kitchen and returned with three plates of food in a tray and set it down on the dining table. Uche was antsy, crying because he was having difficulty returning to his interrupted sleep. I rocked him in my arms till he slept off, laid him in his cot and joined Dan and Victory at the dining table.

After the meal, we returned to the sofa. "How did your day go?" I asked.

"Great. A very funny incident happened, though. A woman came in with labour pains and we were monitoring her. Labour was progressing very well until the point of delivery."

"And?" I edged closer to him, transferring Victory from his laps to mine, to give him room to gesticulate.

"The woman ran out of the labour room. She said the pain was unbearable." He waved both arms in the air indicating the speed with which the woman ran out of the room.

I could not suppress my laughter. "Was that her first baby?" I asked, still laughing.

"Surprisingly, no. It was her fifth pregnancy."

"Fifth? And she is just discovering that labour is painful? So, what did you do?"

"The matron and I pursued her down the corridor. We caught up with her at the end of the corridor and she delivered immediately. A beautiful baby girl. There in the corridor. It wasn't until after we delivered the placenta that we took her inside the ward."

By now, we were all reeling with laughter. "This one na real drama!"

"No be small drama o! We had to send people away from the corridor to give her some form of privacy. Nothing wey person no go see for this Lagos."

Time passed as we traded stories of the strange things, we had experienced in Lagos churches, markets, parties and other places. Soon, Victory drifted off to sleep. Dan rose to leave. "Thanks for the meal. It was awesome. It is probably the thing I miss most about you."

"You are most welcome." I found myself wishing he could stay a little longer. "You said on the phone that you wanted to show me something."

"Ahhh. Yes."

He brought a small box from his pocket. As he opened it, a gasp escaped my lips. At the centre of the pitch-black velvet lining the box was a diamond ring.

"What do you think?" he asked.

"Perfect... emm... Very, very beautiful," I said, touching the rock adorning the ring.

"I was planning on giving this to Bola when she returns from her trip. Do you think she will say yes?" There was anxiety in his voice.

I placed my hand on his shoulder, "She will be the biggest fool in the world if she doesn't."

He smiled and gave me a hug.

After I closed the door behind him, I wiped the tears coming to my eyes and tried hard to smile. Victory was already fast asleep on the rug, so I carried her into the bedroom. I watched the kids sleep, their faces occasionally forming faint smiles. It struck me how much they had made my life worthwhile.

Dan may have found love. But in these children, I found joy.

THIRTY-THREE

"Armoured car, Shelling machine, Heavy artillery. *Ha enweghi ike imeri Biafra!*"

I watched with amusement as Dan's father sang with gusto. Dan had invited me to their family house and made me promise him I would come. I had turned down previous invitations. This time, he used Victory to get to me. Every fifteen minutes, like an alarm clock, she repeated "Mummy, you promised to take us to Unkuyu Dan's house." I could not refuse.

Their Amuwo-Odofin family residence looked the same except for a greenish tint on the fence. I knocked at the black gate.

"Madam Stella, welcome," the gateman greeted, smiling, as he opened the gate. I was surprised that Abdul could still recognize me. He was a grown man now, and he sported a beard covering his entire jaw.

"Abdul, *sanu! Ina kwana?*" I greeted.

"Ah! *Lafia.*" He looked pleased that I was asking after his welfare in his mother tongue. "Kai Madam! Your pikin dem fine well well o."

Dan's father, an amiable man who was in his seventies, was seated on the sofa when we entered. Everyone called him 'Old Major' because of his wartime stories. On seeing me, he sprang up.

"Stella *nwa m*. Long time, no see," he said, as I hugged him. "So you ran away from us, eh?"

"Papa, not really," I said, looking away.

He picked Victory up and carried her in his arms. Delighted, she peered at his spectacles and tried to touch them. I loosened the wrapper tied around my chest, my left hand bringing Uche forward from where he had been secured behind me.

"Your kids are beautiful."

He set Victory down and carried Uche. "Daniel went to pick something from the supermarket. He will be back shortly."

The room was unchanged save for the plasma TV hanging on the opposite wall. Picture frames were arranged adjacent to the floor on all four corners. Victory had walked over to one and was staring at it intently.

"Mummy, is that Unkuyu Dan?" she asked, pointing at the picture. I shot a glance at Old Major and we laughed.

"No, Sweetheart," he volunteered. "That was me as a Major in the Biafran Army, during the war."

"What is war?" Victory asked, turning to me. I was at a loss on how to explain 'war' to a three year old. I was born long after the civil war. "War is when soldiers fight."

That was when Old Major burst into the songs. The way he altered his pitch made his singing sound funny. By the time he was done, Victory was laughing.

"It is a miracle that I am still alive," he said. "I almost died."

"What happened?" I asked, sitting up.

"I was in charge of the troops sent to reclaim Umuahia when it fell. Nigerian soldiers had taken total control of the city. We had perfected plans to launch a surprise counter-attack but somehow our plans were leaked to them by a saboteur." He shook his head, adjusting his glasses. "They were waiting, ready for us.

We were beaten black and blue in broad daylight. Surrounded, with no escape route."

His voice dipped and took on a sad tone. "Bullets were flying, and we were shelled from left and right. The last thing I remembered was an explosion near me. I woke up weeks later in a hospital in Ivory Coast. The doctors told me I was found, covered by the sand, after three days. The rest of the troops were dead." He had tears in his eyes.

My heart broke for those young men who lost their lives to the brutal war.

"Who found you?" I asked.

"Some Biafran soldiers. Usually, after a battle, some soldiers are dispatched for 'combing'. They search the dead soldiers for valuables like guns, ammunition, uniforms. One of the soldiers tripped over the sole of my boot. He proceeded to pull me out of the sand and to his surprise, I sneezed. Then, he saw my rank and with the help of others, carried me to safety."

The door opened. It was Dan. Victory ran to him.

"Finally," he said with a mischievous grin. "Papa, you remember Stella?"

"Your first wife? Sure."

I doubled over in laughter.

"Sorry I can't stay much longer," Old Major said, standing. "I am already late for my meeting." He hurried off into his bedroom to change what he was wearing. When he re-emerged, he tousled Victory's hair, gave her a crisp five hundred naira note for biscuits, and beamed as Abdul locked the gate.

Dan excused himself and returned carrying a tray of drinks. Uche started crying and I brought out his feeding bottle.

"So how did it go? The proposal?" I asked, finally.

"Ah, well," he replied. "I have not found the appropriate time to do that."

"What?" I asked, amused but also surprised. "Which kain cock and bull story be that? Ehn Dan?"

"Bola just returned last week and we both have been very busy," he said, his eyes on the floor.

I knew he was just making excuses. The Dan I knew always created time for things he deemed important. "What is the problem?"

"Nothing o! No problem at all."

"Really? Then why are you dragging your feet?"

He smiled and looked into my face.

"I am not dragging my feet. I just want to be one hundred percent sure."

"Oh. Can one be hundred percent sure? Delay is giving the devil some space. No allow dilly-dallying put sand-sand inside your *garri* o."

He convulsed with laughter. When we dated, he always thought my pidgin English was funny. But right now, I was serious. "Not a laughing matter. From all you have told me, she is a nice, caring and homely girl. She loves you. I have seen her picture and she fine, scatter. Wetin be your problem?"

Dan leaned back on the sofa, smiling. "You are right," he said, standing up. "No further delays."

He brought out his phone and dialled a number. "Hello, Sweetheart." He listened for a bit and said, "Oh, wow. Like minds. Come on in, I have something to show you." And then he hung up.

"What are you doing?" I asked, surprised.

"The proposal, of course. Let me get the ring." He disappeared into the adjoining room. I swallowed hard for lack of words. My heart was a catalogue of emotions, discontent glued to every page. Eight years ago, we had dreamt of happily ever after, in each other's arms. Life happened and incinerated those dreams. Yes, I wanted the best for him, and had encouraged him, but seeing him go about it like this made me feel a type of way. I tried to stand, but felt a little dizzy as I balanced Uche on my back.

Dan emerged clutching the ring case. He shot me a surprised look.

"I need to get going… before… before she comes." The word stumbled off my tongue.

Just then, the door opened. A tall, beautiful girl in a navy blue gown entered. The scent of her perfume filled the room. She seemed puzzled by the sight of me and my children. The surprise on her face cleared when she saw Dan.

"Hello," she said, waving at Victory.

"Sweetheart, meet Stella," Dan said.

"Oh!" She flashed a set of pristine teeth. "You're Stella?" she asked, looking at Dan. He nodded.

"Stella, meet Bolarinwa."

I forced a smile as we shook hands. Her hand was soft and warm. Our gaze met and lingered for a brief second.

My heart sank.

THIRTY-FOUR

"Bola, will you marry me?"

I was still shaking Bola's hand when, without any warning, Dan went down on one knee and popped the question.

For ten whole seconds, the living room was silent and every pair of eyes was on Bola. She was in shock. Her palms were clasped over her mouth as she looked on, dazed. Dan's voice punctured the silence.

"Bolarinwa, will you marry me?" he asked again, this time louder.

At that moment, I wished the past eight years had not happened. I felt like going back in time and undoing the day I met Jide and erase that encounter forever. A part of me wished that Dan's question would go unanswered.

Bola's shriek interrupted my thoughts. "Yes! Yes, Daniel Olisa. I will marry you!" She was ecstatic as she hugged Dan and kissed him. She gave me a hug and then pecked Uche and Victory on their foreheads.

"Congratulations, Dan," I said, forcing a smile. "You two will make an amazing couple."

"Thanks, Stella," he said, embracing me. "Thanks for everything."

As Abdul closed the gate behind us as we left, I took the thrashing I deserved. Compound fool. You thought you could have your cake and still eat it. Stop misplacing your expectations. You have made your choices. Learn to live with them.

"Mummy, come let's bathe Baby." Victory tugged at my wrapper as I prepared dinner.

"You. You should get ready to bathe. But we have to eat first. Have you done your homework?"

She shook her head.

"Ok. We will do it after bathing Baby."

In a trot, she ran out of the kitchen. Why did they always run, children? Was it an innate restlessness or a ready outlet for pent-up energy?

'Bathing Baby' had become Victory's favourite activity. She stood beside the big plastic basin as I bathed Uche, looking on with glee as the water cascaded down the body of the infant. Sometimes, she smeared her hands with soap and rubbed it on Uche's tummy, causing him to giggle.

After bathing, she stroked his soft hair while I applied oil on his skin.

I undressed her afterwards for her own bath while Uche lay in the cot, playing with some toys. Dressed up in her pyjamas, I told her folktales about *mbe nwaniga*, a string of stories my own father told me while growing up, about the exploits of the tortoise. Most times, she fell asleep before the end of the story and I kissed her small frame goodnight. Some nights, she would be wide awake, forcing me to tell another story. Sometimes, I ran out of stories and had to invent new ones with haphazard story lines.

Motherhood was a hard chore. But, I enjoyed that it made me creative.

The children were worth all the stress.

THIRTY-FIVE

"Your CD4 count is very high and your other test results look good."

I had gone for my routine medical check-up and to collect my antiretroviral medications. The doctor smiled as he gave me the good news. "Your body is really kicking this virus. Whatever it is you are doing, just keep it up."

I thanked him and headed towards the dispensary to collect my meds.

The HIV Clinic was situated in a separate, newly-built bungalow, complete with consulting rooms, laboratories and a dispensary. The doctors and nurses working there were nice and empathetic. Prior to seeing a doctor, the nurses would organise a teaching forum for the patients, where HIV/AIDS was explained: modes of transmission, symptoms, testing and the importance of taking one's medications regularly. Questions were asked and clarifications given.

"Your baby is so cute," the young girl beside me said. "How old is he?"

"One year," I replied, smiling. "I am Stella."

"Habiba," she said, touching Uche's cheeks. The boy smiled.

She was wearing a multi-coloured hijab over a dress made from yellow *ankara*.

"Your dress is amazing," I said. "Where did you make it?"

"I made it in Kano before coming."

"I am a tailor. I can make this." I touched the hijab to feel the fabric. Silk.

"Really? I have been looking for one since I came to Lagos. How good are you?" We both laughed at the question.

"Very, very good, believe me," I said. "How long have you been on the meds?"

"All my life," she said, smiling.

"How come? How old are you?"

"Twenty-one. I got the virus from my Mom when she was pregnant with me. Testing was rare those days and meds were scarce. She passed on soon after I was born. My dad ensured I started getting the meds early enough."

"Eeya. *Pele*," I said, in sympathy.

"For what?" she asked, laughing. "See, having this virus has turned out to be a blessing in disguise. Living with HIV has made me appreciate life more and make the best use of every given opportunity. I just graduated with a First Class in Law from the University and currently, I'm doing my Law School Programme in Lagos. It remains a blessing for me to this day."

Her courage was baffling. Our stories couldn't have been more dissimilar. At twenty-one, she was already an academic giant. At twenty-one, I met the man that gave me HIV. She saw her affliction as a blessing. Mine left me in pieces - a shattered porcelain plate.

"Habiba Usman!" a voice called from the dispensary. She entered and soon emerged with her meds. She handed me an envelope, embroidered with a fine gold thread.

"My wedding invitation. Next month. Promise me you will come."

"Where?"

"Here in Lagos. Let me have your number. I will check out your shop." We exchanged contacts.

"I will try and attend," I said, standing to go and pick my meds. "You are phenomenal."

I left the hospital in high spirits. Something had shifted. Habiba was a testament that most of our limitations were self-imposed.

Everything was possible.

THIRTY-SIX

"Ma-Ma."

I had just finished feeding Uche and was stroking his back when he made those historic sounds. His first words.

"Ma-Ma," I heard him again, my heart awash with emotions.

"Vicky! Baby just talked."

Victory abandoned her dinner and ran to where I was sitting. She started tickling the baby to get him to talk again. Uche laughed and then made a crying face.

"Okay, okay," I said, standing up to console the baby. Talk time was over.

At three months, Uche could control his neck and hold his head upright. Prior to that, I would place a hand behind his head when I carried him to avoid a sudden backward tilt. After six months, he was able to remain in a sitting position with minimal swaying. Two lower teeth sprouted the following month. It was also around that period that he fell ill.

I woke up one night to discover that he was having a fever. He was also passing frequent watery stools. Concerned, I carried him to Mama Tunde's house.

"Ah! His problem is teething. Just give him these drugs and he will be fine," she said, handing me three plastic bottles. I was unconvinced. Victory had gone through her teething phase, but she had not exhibited such a worrying illness. However, I knew better than to disagree with Mama Tunde. I thanked her and left.

At home, I checked the bottles she had given me. One had 'Teething Mixture' written in bold. The others looked strange. I picked up my phone and called Dan.

"I think he is just having acute watery diarrhoea," he said, after listening to my complaints. "Bring him over to the hospital tomorrow and don't give him those 'teething mixtures'. You can give him liquid paracetamol for the fever, if you have it. Or you can clean the body with a towel soaked in warm water. It will reduce the fever."

I thanked him.

The next morning, I took Uche to the hospital. After examining the baby, the doctor prescribed Oral Rehydration Solution. I was given three sachets and the nurse taught me how to mix it with water. When I gave it to the Baby, it worked like magic. The diarrhoea and the fever disappeared.

The next evening, I went to see Mama Tunde.

"Iya Vicky, how is the baby?"

"He is very fine now. I came to return the drugs. *E se pupo!*"

"I told you they will work," she said with a satisfied smile.

I couldn't bring myself to burst her bubble of satisfaction.

She meant well.

THIRTY-SEVEN

A black Range Rover SUV pulled up outside my shop. We waited to see the occupants, the noise of the sewing machines dying down for a moment. The rear door opened and a woman wearing a brown hijab came down. My face lit up as I saw her.

"Habiba! Na you be this?" I asked, smiling. Her face was glowing.

"Ahn ahn! Stella. I told you I will come nau."

I offered her a seat. "We thought it was one big politician o!" I said, motioning at the car parked outside.

"Don't mind my fiancé. He insisted on bringing me himself."

She looked around the room, admiring some finished clothes. Her eyes soon fell on Uche, who was crawling at one end of the shop. She went over to carry him.

"How's the preparation coming? It's next weekend, abi? Your wedding?" I asked.

"Yup. Next weekend."

She went through my catalogue and chose some designs she liked. I took her measurements.

"Can you make fine hijabs?" she asked, as I measured her bust.

"Yes. I can make some lovely hijabs to go with the designs you chose, using silk, cotton or even chiffon materials."

"I prefer silk." "Noted," I said, writing down her measurements in my notebook. "Why do Muslim women always cover up?"

She smiled. "It helps keep our beauty under wraps. The Quran instructs that we should not display our beauty to outside males. Only one's husband and close relatives should see such beauty on display. For me, it is both an identity and a fashion statement."

"You also pray five times daily?"

She laughed. "Of course. Every good Muslim prays five times a day."

"Interesting."

Habiba and I concluded on the designs and the price. She rose to leave and I accompanied her. The SUV was parked further down the street. Out of earshot of anyone else, I asked her a question that had been bothering me. "Is your fiancé also on antiretrovirals?"

"No. He is negative."

"Wow. Is he aware of your status?"

"Yes. I told him early in our courtship. He had his period of conflict. Men always do when you tell them the unpleasant truth about yourself. He had a doctor friend who understood how much he loved me and reassured him that a marriage between us will be possible without him getting infected."

"How?" We had stopped a small distance from the car.

"Since I have been on antiretroviral medications for a long time, my viral load is very, very low. So are my chances of infecting anyone. The doctor said that if we decide to have a baby, we can meet unprotected only during my ovulation period. That way, I can still conceive and if I continue on the drugs, I can give birth to an HIV negative baby."

"It sounds very doable," I said, nodding.

As we approached the car, the tinted glass on the driver's side came down. A man in an army uniform smiled at me as he opened the door. At the centre of his chest, he had a badge with three black stars.

"Dalha, this is Stella, my tailor and very good friend," Habiba said. "Stella, meet Dalha, my soldier love." She added, laughing.

Dalha shook my hand. His grip was firm.

"I will try and attend your wedding. Habiba will send me directions," I said.

"We will be expecting you," he said.

As they drove off, I stood on the road watching the car recede into the distance.

Knowledge is indeed, power.

THIRTY-EIGHT

As I approached my shop the next morning, a girl rested against the wall beside the door. Young, she looked like she was in her late teens and wore a loose-fitting blue blouse over denim jeans. A new customer, perhaps.

She greeted me as I opened the locks. "Good morning, Ma."

"Good morning, dear. You want to see me?"

"Yes."

I ushered her into the shop and motioned her to sit. The room was stuffy so I opened the windows. Uche stirred on my back. My movements had woken him. I loosened the wrapper tied across my chest and cradled him, resting his head on my bosom.

"So which kind of cloth do you want to make?" I asked her.

She was silent. After some time, she spoke up. "I am not here to make a dress. I came... I came to talk about... about the baby." Her gaze was fixed on the floor.

"Which baby?"

"My baby. The one you are carrying."

She would wish she never made that statement. I set Uche down on a wrapper and in one moment of blind rage, I bundled her out of my shop. "If I ever see you here again, eh! Rubbish!"

She was sobbing outside as some persons passing by stood and watched. I had gone from zero to one hundred in a finger snap and I never knew I had that in me. I hurried back into the shop and met Uche crying. Carrying him, I rocked him till he stopped.

"Who is that small girl outside?" Ebele asked as she entered. "She was crying and kept pointing at our shop."

I was too angry to respond.

The events of that morning marred my day. I pedaled the sewing machine, wiping away the tears that came to my eyes. She came to talk about the baby. What guts!

By noon, I took a break to feed Uche. In between mouthfuls, he would break into a smile, baring his scanty dentition. I smiled in return.

"Aunty Stella," Ebele said, directing her gaze to the door. I looked up from where I was sitting.

An elderly couple entered the shop. Right behind them was the girl from the morning. My rage returned. In a split second, I was on my feet. "Didn't I tell you that I don't want to set my eyes on you?"

"Praise, please wait outside," the elderly man told the girl.

She stepped outside.

"Madam, please calm down," the woman began. "We are not here to make any trouble."

The couple sat down. I struggled to stay calm, my arms wrapped around Uche.

"We don't really know where to begin," the man started. "We buried our only son last week."

His face had deep furrows and his grey hair told of a man who had seen life.

"I am Chief Adewale Tikolo and this is my wife, Lametan. Jimmy, our son, was a final year Engineering student at the University of Lagos before his death. On the night of Monday, last week, some suspected cultists went to his off-campus residence and shot my Jimmy dead." His voice shook. The woman let out a whimper.

"I was called by one of his friends. When we got there, my Jimmy had ten bullet wounds and was lying in a pool of his own blood."

"He died in my arms," the woman added, amidst sobs. "Before we reached the hospital, he was dead."

The man continued. "Yesterday evening, the girl outside, Praise, visited our house. We've never seen her before. She said she was in the same University with Jimmy. That she was his girlfriend. We didn't know what to make of the information until she told us that she had a child for Jimmy.

At first, we didn't believe the story. Jimmy never told us about getting anyone pregnant. We called some of his friends and they all admitted that they knew the girl. Two of his friends knew of the pregnancy. They said Jimmy denied the pregnancy."

"Praise! Come inside," the woman said.

The girl entered, avoiding my gaze.

"Tell us exactly what happened," the man ordered her.

She was fidgeting. "When I found out I was pregnant, I told Jimmy. He told me to stop the joke. When he realized that I was serious, he broke down and told me he was not ready to be a father. The next day, he gave me some money for an abortion. He said that his parents were elders in the church and that the news of my pregnancy would embarrass the family."

The couple shifted in their seats.

"When I refused to have an abortion, he grew very angry and accused me of trying to trap him with a pregnancy. He stopped picking my calls. The last time

I visited his house, he threw me out and told me to go to whoever was responsible for the pregnancy. I was heart-broken when I left his house. I could not tell my parents. I was still in my first year at the university, far away from home and confused. I confided in one of my fellowship sisters, a final year student. She encouraged me and helped me during the pregnancy.

I left school when the pregnancy was six months old. I spent the next three months hiding in her house. She graduated before I was due to give birth and left for youth service the week I put to bed. I was alone again, accompanied by the endless cry of the poor child I brought to this world. One day, I could not bear it any longer. I dropped the baby at Olaitan Street, near the refuse dump."

"You little devil." I fought the urge to give her a resounding slap. "Where is the baby now? Where?" I asked.

"I saw you pick him up. And I followed you at a distance as you went home," she said, looking at me. "I have seen you many times with the baby. I have never had the courage to approach you. I have felt guilt and emptiness since that night. So, when I heard that Jimmy was dead, I felt I should let the parents know that they have a grandchild."

"This is my Jimmy." The woman handed me a photograph.

I was not expecting what I saw, and it disarmed me. The picture was that of a handsome young man. He was fair, tall and smiling at the camera, looking out at the world with the confidence of one who had a fruitful life ahead of him.

Uche was his spitting image.

THIRTY-NINE

"Dan, I need help," I said, and hung up as fast as I had dialed. He was trying to say something. But it didn't matter. Nothing did. I was in a very dark place.

For three days, I was drowning in an ocean of sadness. The thought of anyone coming for my baby was unbearable. It started with the visit from Jimmy's parents. I had locked up the shop after they left, dismissing everyone. I went to pick up Victory at her school and we headed home.

As the weekend wore on, I grew more and more despondent. Victory must have noticed something was wrong because she kept to herself, talking to her doll. Uche cried less and slept more. I went through the motions, preparing their meals. My appetite was gone, as had my interest in everything. I sat in the bed from morning till night, holding Uche in my arms. My mind was a broken tape recorder, rehashing thousands of questions, all of which filled me with anger and dread.

I was sinking fast and I knew the only reasonable thing was to make that call. A flurry of text messages entered my phone as I dropped the call. Three were from Habiba. One contained directions for the wedding the following weekend. She had come to the shop with Dalha on Saturday and found it locked. She wanted to know whether I had finished any of her clothes. One was from my sister, Nkechi. She was trying to check up on me. I switched off the phone.

I heard a knock on the door. Then, a second knock came. As I went to answer the door, I took a quick glance at my living room. It was in disarray.

It didn't matter.

"Who is it?" I asked.

"Stella, it is me. Dan."

I opened the door to let him in.

"What's wrong?" he asked, his voice tinged with worry.

"They came to… they wanted to…take Uche." Tears were streaming freely from my eyes.

"Who are they? And where is Vicky?"

"She is inside. Vicky, Uncle Dan is here!" I called out, wiping away the tears with my wrapper. She emerged from the room and greeted him. There was no excitement in her voice.

I told Dan everything. When I was done, he looked disturbed. "No no! They can't do that. They can't take the baby away. Let me call Bola. She is a lawyer. I think we need to know what the law says in this matter." He turned away to make the phone call.

"Mummy, is anyone taking Baby away?" Victory asked, holding Uche's left arm. I had forgotten she was present when I was talking to Dan.

"No, Sweetheart. Nobody is taking Baby away," I said, stroking her head.

"Bola is on her way back from work. She will stop over," Dan said.

He left and returned after some time with Bola. She was dressed in a spotted white shirt and a black suit. The sound of her shoe heels interrupted the silence in the room. She greeted me and asked me to tell her everything. I narrated everything, starting from the night I picked Uche from beside the refuse bin.

"After you picked up the baby, did you make any move to formally adopt him?" she asked.

"Like how?" I asked, confused.

"Did you go to any Social Welfare Department to begin the adoption process?"

"No. I went to the Police Station. They collected my statement and sent us away. I never knew about Social Welfare."

"Hmmm." She shook her head. "Going to the Police clears you from any accusation of child kidnapping. But you ought to have begun the adoption process."

I was indignant. "I didn't know. I had no idea there was a Social Welfare department."

"Ignorance of the law is no excuse."

Her words stung.

The room was silent again. I was distraught. Victory shuffled her feet. I looked at Bola. "Please, can you help stop them from taking my baby away?"

"I will try. But your case is weak. Granted, Praise may be ruled unfit to raise Uche. But what about his grandparents, to whom he is related by blood?" She was blunt and at that moment, I hated that about her.

"Okay. Enough of the crying and moodiness," Dan said, standing. "No one is taking the baby away. Not today." He turned to me. "Get everyone dressed. We are going out."

He tickled Victory. Her eyes lit up as she laughed.

"I am not in the mood to go anywhere," I said.

"I was not asking."

Thirty minutes later, the cold blast from air-conditioners welcomed us as we took our seats in Mr. Biggs. Their fried, tenderized chicken did much to restore my appetite. Victory, who was licking her ice-cream, casted glances at the children having fun in the play section, before going over to join them.

Bola ate in silence, but I sensed she was studying me.

"So, how was work today? Any highlights?" I asked Dan.

"Highlights? Let's see. OK, something strange happened this evening," Dan said, setting down his glass of orange juice. "An elderly man was brought to the mortuary. He was said to have died in his sleep in the morning."

Bola and I listened with rapt attention.

"The mortician pierced the 'dead' man's neck to introduce formalin and noticed something strange. Fresh blood flowed. The man grabbed his arm. After an intense struggle, the mortician broke free and fled, screaming."

"What is formalin?" Bola asked.

"It is a liquid chemical used to preserve dead bodies," Dan said. "Anyway, one of the security men held the fleeing mortician down, and people gathered. The news spread and some security men decided to go back with him to verify. Lo and behold, the 'dead' man was standing at the entrance of the mortuary, bleeding from his neck. Everyone took to their heels. The 'dead' man was walking around the hospital. A nurse saw him bleeding and took him to the Accident and Emergency section. The wound was closed. He had suffered some kind of memory loss and could not remember how he got to the hospital. His people were called. You need to see the shock on their faces when they saw him."

Bola was laughing. "So, would one say he rose up from the dead?" she asked.

"Maybe he wasn't dead in the first place. We are still struggling to explain what happened," Dan said.

"Maybe it is a miracle," I said, smiling. "Death looks final. But God can turn even death around. He can give us back our lives just as he did for that man."

We dispersed after the meal, my mood lifted.

FORTY

"Why do men cheat?" Ebele asked as she cut a lace material on the table. I paused to look at her and couldn't suppress my laughter.

"Aunty, why are you laughing? Is it not an important question to ask?"

"It is important o!" I said, still laughing. "When you see men, help me ask them."

We were swamped with work and I was hurrying to meet some deadlines. Habiba's wedding was the next day and I had promised her the clothes would be ready by that evening. I didn't want to disappoint her.

I stood up to stretch my back. The standing fan in the room blew hot air in my direction and I sighed. It was that time of the year when the sun fires down with rage, as though angry with mankind. The rains had not started and everywhere, people complained about the heat. I picked up a pair of scissors and trimmed off the excess thread from one of Habiba's hijabs. Her clothes were almost finished.

"My landlord and his wife had a big fight in our compound today," Ebele said. She lived in a block of flats, twelve rooms in two wings facing each other.

"Again?" I asked, amused. "Don't they ever get tired?"

"Hmmm. The fight this time was very serious o! The man was having his bath when his phone rang. The wife picked the call. It was a woman. Na so the wife begin interrogate the woman. As soon as the husband came out of the bathroom, she confronted him. The next thing we knew, they were shouting at the top of their voices, throwing accusations back and forth. Next thing, dem don begin fight. Dem fight comot the house and continued at the centre of the compound. Their children were trying to separate them. Dem no gree."

I shook my head. "So, how the fight take end?"

"The woman brought a pestle and took aim at the man. The man dodged it and landed her a blow on the head, with his fist. The woman fainted. Na so me I pick race begin come shop, because if Police come, dem go arrest everybody. As I was leaving, the children were pouring cold water on her, trying to revive her. The man just sat on a chair, fanning himself."

"*Tufiakwa!*" I snapped my fingers. "In his mind he is one heavyweight champion, abi?"

Ebele hissed. "I still don't understand why a man will cheat on the mother of his children."

"Men are complicated beings. Their minds don't work like ours. A man can just leave his mistress' apartment and go straight home to his wife and children, feeling no qualms. Some men cheat because they are bored. Some cheat because they feel that they can. But the majority cannot explain why they cheat. I think cheating is a bad habit some men picked from the past before they got married. A few kick the habit by becoming more disciplined and God-fearing. The rest just keep doing till one day when monkey go go market, e no go return."

Uche started crying, his way of announcing he was awake. He had been sleeping on the floor at one end of the room. Ebele paused her work and brought him to me. His cries reduced as I soothed him before I fetched his feeding bottle and began to feed him.

I had tried not to think of the events of the past week. Jimmy's parents had offered to meet with me several times, but I refused. I avoided anything that could take me back into that dark place. I tried to be happy, burying myself in work and loving my kids.

Just then, Ola, my student tailor, entered the shop with Victory. She'd helped me to pick her up from school.

"Mummy!" Victory ran over to where I was working, with Uche on my lap.

"V-Darling, how was school today?" I said, setting Uche down on a wrapper.

"Fine," she said, as she shrugged her school bag off her back. I ran my hand through her braids and stroked her cheek. She smiled. Her yellow checkered uniform had a brown sandy spot at the hem.

I opened her lunch box. Her food was untouched.

"Why didn't you eat your food?" I asked her. She was quiet. "Oya, carry this food now and go and finish it. I don't want to see one grain of rice remaining."

She picked up the lunch box and moved towards the fan.

I worked in silence for another two hours. By 5.15pm, I stood up in triumph. Habiba's clothes were complete, so I called to tell her that they were ready.

She entered the shop thirty minutes later, in the company of an older woman. Her hands were covered with intricate designs in black ink.

"*Amariya*," I said, smiling. "Your work give me wahala o!"

She laughed. "I am happy you finished it. You tailors know how to disappoint pesin eh!" She turned to the woman with her. "This is my friend, Stella. She owns this shop." She faced me. "Aisha is my cousin's wife.

They all came for the wedding."

I greeted the woman who seemed more interested in the children sleeping on a spread-out wrapper at the far end of the room.

"Are they your kids?" she asked, pointing at Victory and Uche.

"Yes," I replied, separating Habiba's clothes from the pile of finished work.

"How long have you been married?" she asked again.

"I...*um*...am not married," I said.

She gave me a look I couldn't place. I shrugged.

"You are a lucky woman."

"How?"

"I've been married for ten years. And I'm yet to have a child." There was pain in her voice.

"My husband went ahead and married a second wife. Then, a third, followed by a fourth wife. None of us have given him a child. I am praying, *insha Allah*, that I will be the first one to give him an heir. And here you are, with two children. Two!" Two of her fingers were in my face.

"Have you been to a hospital? At least, to know what is wrong?" I asked, touched by her plight.

"No," she said. "I mentioned it once. My husband dismissed the idea."

"Hmmm. I think you should go to the hospital. They may be able to help you there. Habiba should be able to take you." I said.

"I can't go without my husband's permission," she said, facing the wall.

I woke the children after the women had left the shop. Ebele and Ola said their goodbyes and left for the day. I locked the shop, with Uche safely strapped to my back and Victory standing by, sleepy-eyed.

We walked down the busy street that led to my house, my heart filled with gratitude for the blessing squirming on my back and the other clasping my hand. A part of my mind hummed like a busy sewing machine, trying to grasp why a grown woman like Aisha needed permission from her husband to seek treatment.

The worst prisons are not made with iron bars.

FORTY-ONE

The beep from my phone woke me. I squinted at the message icon that danced on the screen and pressed the message button. The message was brief and the tone was terse.

You have been avoiding us.
We have given you enough time.
Please, come with the baby to Chief Tikolo's residence, 13 Alao Crescent, beside 2nd Rainbow junction tomorrow by 12 noon, or face legal action.
Thank you.

I laid back into the bed, tears welling up in my eyes.

It was the morning of Habiba's wedding. Nkechi had agreed to come over and take care of the kids to enable me to attend the wedding. I thrashed about in bed for some time, thinking of a plan. None came. I gazed at the solitary bulb at the center of the ceiling, allowing its light to dispel any beclouding darkness. It had no care in the world.

For a moment, I wished my only purpose was to shine, a simple job with no new responsibilities, bitter memories and pending problems. But such a simple existence would lack love. Could I have coped without the love from my family and loved ones? For all I cared, the bulb envied me.

My lonesome musings were interrupted by a knock on the front door. I stood up and dragged myself to the living room.

"I thought you said you are leaving early for the wedding, eh? You are not even dressed," Nkechi said as she walked past me, into the living room. I closed the door behind her.

"I am not even sure I am still going," I said.

"Why? What is wrong?" she asked, facing me.

I scratched my head. No words came.

"Go and dress up, joor! You don't know you should still be in circulation?" she said, laughing and patting my shoulder.

"*Hapu m aka, biko.* Was I out of circulation before?"

I had kept my sister in the dark about my entire situation. I was avoiding the heart-rending 'I told you so'. She had warned me about Jide, but I was carried away by the euphoria of that moment. She was not aware of my HIV status. I had told no one, except Dan. I had to tell him.

It had not been easy to open up to him. When I was done talking, he stood there, looking at me, saying nothing. I knew I just broke his heart, again. His next action had caught me off-guard. He hugged me and whispered in my ears, "I know he did this. But know that I will be there for you. Always."

The bus dropped me off just after Ikeja Bridge. I took a cab going to Esomo Close through Toyin Street and stopped at the house numbered 10. Outside the compound, several cars were parked. A good number of them had military plate numbers. I entered the compound.

A white duplex stood at the centre with its balcony suspended by two pillars. There were several canopies set up in the compound, with seats arranged under them. I went into the building and asked for Habiba. I was directed upstairs.

"Ah Stella, you made it!" Habiba sprang up, her elegance filling the room. I embraced her, made some remarks about her resplendent look and offered her my congratulations. Aisha and her cousins were dressing Habiba up. She was dazzling, a smile plastered on her face. They were chatting in Hausa, breaking into laughter from time to time. I couldn't follow the conversation. I lingered in the room for a while and became restless, so I excused myself and went downstairs to look around.

There were many people seated in the expansive living room. I found my way to the backyard and sat on one of the empty chairs. A dark young man in blue *kaftan* and a matching cap was seated in one. He was looking at the flowers adjacent to the fence. He looked up as I passed by him, said hello, and sat next to him.

"When is the wedding starting?" I asked him.

"Anytime from now," he said. "The Imam is already here."

He spoke without any accent. I had never met a Hausa man without one.

"I am Stella, a friend of the bride," I said, offering him my hand.

"Ali," he said, shaking my hand. "Friend of the groom and cousin to the bride."

"So Ali," I began, smiling. "Who did you sell your accent to?"

He laughed hard and long. "Oho! Maybe I wasn't at the meeting when it was agreed that we must all have an accent. I bet you also think every Fulani man is a poor cattle rearer."

"No, I don't!" I said. "But most of them are cattle rearers nau?"

"Of course. But they are far from being poor. Don't allow their dressing to fool you."

"Really?" I asked. "How rich could they be?"

"Very, very rich. Some families may have up to fifty thousand cattle, scattered all over the country. Each son may be in charge of a group of ten thousand. How much does one cow cost?"

"About one hundred thousand naira," I said.

"Do the math. That is a total of five billion naira. Yet, you won't see them dress fancy or show off."

I was stunned. I knew I would never look at those nomads I saw chasing cows the same way again.

"What do you do?" he asked.

"I am a tailor or a fashion designer, whichever you prefer." I answered with a smile. "You?"

"I am a banker. I was recently transferred to Lagos from Kaduna. I am still trying to relocate my family."

"You are married?"

He smiled. "Yes. I have four wives."

"Kai!" I could not hide my amazement. "What are you doing with four wives?"

He started laughing again. "The more, the merrier. Besides, it is allowed in Islam."

"Hmmm. You wan born one village ni?" I asked.

He smiled. "We are working on it. Each of my wives has three kids."

He asked for my phone number. I gave it to him, still bemused at the thought of how large his household must be.

Just then, we heard the sound of prayers emerging from the living room. "It seems the Nikkhai just started," Ali said, rising.

As we were entering the building, we met Aisha in the hallway. She looked surprised to see us.

"Mai gida," she said, looking at Ali. "They are asking for you inside."

"This is your husband?" I asked Aisha. She nodded.

"You know my first wife?" Ali asked, looking uneasy.

"Yes. It is really a very small world," I replied, smiling.

The smile had no amusement in it, as I realized he had been lying about all the children his wives had. My memory of what Aisha had told me about her childlessness was still very fresh. Not to mention the disturbing fact that she could not do something as simple as visit a hospital without his permission. A smooth-talking, deceitful slave-master. Truly, being well-spoken does not always translate to being a gentleman.

He was about to say something else but I wasn't in the mood to indulge him.

FORTY-TWO

"Why is there a scarcity of good, marriageable men?" a female passenger from the back row of the bus asked. We were trapped in traffic as I was returning from Habiba's wedding. Sandwiched between two passengers in the second row, my outfit was soaked in perspiration.

Her question prompted mixed reactions from the passengers. The men disagreed while the women nodded in agreement.

"No talk that thing!" the bus conductor hollered. "Na just money dey stop most men. The country is hard and weddings too dey cost these days. Men full everywhere!"

"For where?" The girl who had asked the question insisted. "Almost one quarter of able-bodied men dey prison. Half of the men wey go school are unemployed and have no money to start a home. Na the remaining one-quarter wey una want all the girls to dey drag, abi?" The bus was thrown into laughter.

"I think it is the value system that has changed," an elderly man said. "Present day girls want ready-made men. Unfortunately, most of those men are married. They get involved and before they realize it, the boat has moved." The bus fell silent.

We jerked forward a little as we made the semblance of progress and then, the bus stopped again. I closed my eyes in fatigue.

The day was hectic. Habiba's wedding ceremony had been brief but colourful. After the initial pleasantries, the Imam collected the bride-price from Dalha's parents and handed it to Habiba's father, together with some kolanuts and packets of candies. The bride-price was only thirty thousand naira. After the payment of the bride-price, the Imam declared them husband and wife and prayers were offered on their behalf. I sat quietly in a corner of the room and prayed for the couple in my mind.

One of the highlights of the event for me was the 'Kamun Amariya' which I later learnt to be an old wedding tradition. Aisha and other females surrounded Habiba and members of Dalha's family tried to negotiate her release to them. It was a negotiation, intentionally drawn out for fun, with a lot of back and forth from each family's representatives in Hausa.

I had scanned my mind for a parallel in Igboland. The closest would be negotiating the bride price and the items on the marriage list but that was usually not fun. The only fun equivalent would be the cocky dance by the bride, palmwine-in-hand as she searched for her husband amidst appeals from other young men to hand the cup to them.

Food was served after the Kamun. I noticed I was probably the only single lady in the room. Most of Habiba's relatives were married, a fact that got me thinking. Does polygamy help them in the North to mop up the 'excess' women in circulation? When will the people in the South cut down the financial aspect of marriage requirements to encourage more persons to get married, just like in the North?

Just then, I remembered the text from the morning and let out a big sigh. Tomorrow was just a few hours away. The voices of hawkers announcing their wares interrupted my thoughts. Our bus began another series of slow movements.

"Your *gele* is fine," the man on my left said.

"Thank you," I replied with a smile.

He was dark, dressed in a white native shirt and probably in his mid-thirties. I had been struggling to keep the extra-large headscarf on my head, but after several failed attempts, I removed it altogether.

"Did you tie it yourself?" he asked.

"Yes," I said. "Though I had little help from my sister."

"Na dis one dem dey call 'canopy' abi?" He asked, laughing.

"Not this one," I said. "Na the elder sister."

More laughter.

"I am Timi," he said. "Timipriye."

"From where?" I asked. The name sounded strange.

"Bayelsa. Na we dey sustain this nation with oil."

"Really?"

"Ehen nau! Most oil wells are in our place. The whole economy is built on our oil. Without us this nation would have collapsed since." He had a loud voice and a confident mien, the kind that announced one from a privileged background. His wrist, resting on the metal frame of the seat before us, spotted a fancy watch.

"Hmmm. How did the oil come about?" I asked.

"Many years ago, our grandfathers had a meeting and thought of how to help their children and future generations. So they agreed that when they die and are buried, they will produce oil daily. Till date, my ancestors are working hard, producing oil in the ground, so that we, their children, will not suffer."

I could not suppress my laughter. Some other passengers were also laughing. Timi was smiling with satisfaction.

"So, why is oil not in other places?" I asked, still laughing.

"Maybe their ancestors are lazy. Maybe their ancestors don't care," he said.

The whole bus roared with more laughter.

We reached my bus stop. I collected the balance of my fare from the conductor and walked into my street. My feet dragged as I climbed the staircase and knocked on the door. When the door opened, Dan was at the door, carrying Uche in his arms.

"You look beautiful," he said. "How did the wedding go?"

"The wedding went fine. Thanks. Where is Nkechi?"

"She is at your Aunt's. They called and said it was urgent. I just came by this evening and she told me. I asked her to go."

"Mummy!" Victory ran out from the room.

I carried her. "V-Darling, how have you been?"

"Fine," she said, smiling.

I went into the room to undress and then came out to prepare dinner.

After dinner, I told Dan about the text message. "I am coming with you tomorrow," he said. "We really need to straighten things out with Jimmy's parents."

"You know, I have come to see Uche as my son," I said.

"Maybe that's why it is so painful." He placed a hand on my shoulder. "Everything happens for a reason."

As I saw him off that night, I asked him a question

that had been bothering me.

"Dan, why are you being so nice to me?"

He was silent for a moment. "You would have done the same for me," he began. "You know, I feel so guilty for shutting you out when I did. Maybe if I had not, we would have been in a better place." His voice shook.

I held his hand in reassurance. "I think we are in a better place."

A smile formed on his lips, gladdening my heart.

FORTY-THREE

"What is really going on between you and Dan?"
Bola asked. There was a seriousness in her voice I
hadn't noticed before. I had called to inform her of the
text message I got and my intended visit to the address.
Apparently, Dan had told her that he would accompany
me. I swallowed hard at my end of the line.

"Nothing."

"It better be. I know you two had something in the
past. But that is where it ends, in the past. I am Dan's
present as well as his future. I will not like us to have an
issue over this." The click of the phone as she hung up
echoed in my ears.

I stared at the phone and then threw it on the bed.
Her question had startled me. Was she jealous? If she
had an issue, she should have taken it up with Dan, not
me. Dan always visited me of his own volition and I had
supported her engagement to Dan. How could she
consider me her rival? She was spoiling for war, a war
which I had no strength to fight. The chime of the clock
jolted me back to my senses. 10am. I was running out
of time. I went to get Uche ready.

Dan came around by 10.30 am. He was looking
worried. "I don't know what's wrong with Bola," he
said.

"How?" I asked, my mind racing.

"She was not sounding happy when I called her this
morning and yet when I asked her what was wrong, she
said she was fine. I persisted till it almost sounded like I
was nagging her. She still maintained she was fine."

"Oh! Most times when we say we are 'fine', we really are not. We simply try to draw strength from saying that to enable us to tackle the problem. Maybe you should check on her when we return."

"Sure, I will. Are we ready to leave?"

"Yes."

I didn't mention Bola's call to me to avoid adding gasoline to a smoldering fire. Downstairs, we dropped Victory at Mama Tunde's house to play with her children while we were away.

The address was not hard to locate. We stood in front of the gate and knocked. A security guard opened the gates, greeted us and pointed us to the main building. It was a brown duplex with a driveway just in front of the main entrance. Inside, the living room we entered was spacious, with black leather sofas arranged in a semicircle.

Chief Tikolo was seated when we entered, but stood up when he saw us. "Ah! Thank you very much for coming," he greeted, then motioned us to sit. I sat down, cradling Uche in my arms. The seat was soft, softer than any leather sofa I had ever settled onto before, but I hid my awe. I did not want them to think I was intimidated by their obvious wealth. His wife emerged from an adjacent room and greeted us with a smile. "Una welcome o!"

I looked around the room. Jimmy's pictures hung on the wall. Baby pictures, birthday pictures, and a matriculation picture, with both parents flanking him.

We were soon joined by two elderly men. One was introduced as the Senior Pastor in their church. The other was the family lawyer.

"We appreciate you all for making it to this meeting," the Senior Pastor said. "God in his infinite wisdom and inscrutable ways has decided to console this family, who recently lost their only son, with a grandson. Despite the circumstances surrounding his birth, his survival up to this moment is a testimony that this child was sent to wipe away the tears from the eyes of these two servants of God." He pointed at Jimmy's parents.

Chief Tikolo spoke next. "Stella, we have been trying to meet you. Not to make trouble. No. Not at all. The fact that this baby is alive today is just because of you. You really possess the milk of human kindness. You are a candidate for heaven."

I felt my eyes moisten.

He continued. "You fed, clothed and provided for a child whom you picked up from the street. Raising children is very difficult. But you did this, single-handedly."

His wife came and knelt before me. I protested but she held my knees. "We appreciate the kindness and love you have lavished on this baby," she said. "I am your fellow woman. My only son, whom I suckled, is no more. This baby is the only hope we have left. Please, allow us to raise him. Please. Please." She was sobbing. Everyone in the room had their eyes fixed on me. I opened my mouth to talk but no words came out. My tears flowed without restraint. I closed my eyes for a moment, wiping the moisture from them with the back of my hands. I looked at Uche. His face was expressionless. In an instant, flashes of our journey together hit me: his smiles, giggles and babbling, his first words. I felt his smooth skin and ran my hands through his luxuriant hair.

The room remained silent. Mrs. Tikolo was still kneeling before me. A third of her hair was gray and wrinkles were etched on her forehead.

Chief Tikolo broke the silence. "Here is a cheque for one million naira. We know it is nothing but you can have it for all the troubles the baby may have caused you."

"No, no, no," I said, shaking my head.

"Please, take it," he insisted.

"Sir, with all due respect, Uche is my son. He has been my son since the day I picked him from the refuse dump and I have treated him as such. I never knew this day would come."

My voice trailed off. I was crying. Dan held my shoulders.

"I will always consider him my son. Whatever I did for him, was done out of love. I cannot accept any amount of money for that."

"Will you allow us to raise him?" his wife asked, looking up. Her eyes were expectant.

I fought back my tears and turned to Dan. His face was blank. I knew that the decision was up to me. Summoning every ounce of energy in me and suppressing my screaming maternal instincts, I said the one word that would change their lives.

"Yes."

FORTY-FOUR

I woke up in the middle of the night and went to the cot. It was empty. My mouth parted in alarm before my brain restored some parts of the dreaded memory. Uche was gone. Slumping into the bed, my ribs racked with sobs. How did I let this happen? How did I let my bundle of joy slip through my fingers? How could I let go without a fight?

For two days, Victory barely ate and refused to speak to me. That was after her question "Mummy, where is Baby?" was met with an empty stare. I tried to explain, but it was not making sense to her. Rounds after rounds of explanation, and she would still ask where Baby was. I decided that any explanation without producing Baby was useless.

She grew sullen and withdrawn. I was too broken to be bothered. My mind kept replaying the events of that afternoon, wishing I could take it all back.

As soon as I had agreed to allow them raise Uche, the Tikolos jubilated. Mrs. Tikolo stood up and hugged me. Her husband joined in the embrace.

"My daughter, you just gave us a new life," he said, beaming with smiles.

His wife was effusive with gratitude and stretched her arms to carry the baby. I withdrew. Holding the baby, I watched his tummy rise and fall with every breath. How could a person so small be so powerful? He had been my lifeline. Now, he was the cause of their joy.

Dan sat in silence through it all, the only one not swept away by the euphoria in the room. The Senior Pastor was jubilant. The family lawyer who had barely spoken since the introduction did not let his stutter stop him. "Th-th-th-thank you."

"You will always be welcome in our home," Chief Tikolo said. "You can visit the baby anytime. You are his mother and hence, our daughter."

Overwhelmed, I struggled to keep my emotions in check.

"You can go home and bring him tomorrow," he said. "I know this must be very hard for you."

Teary-eyed, I thanked them and we left.

Outside the gate, Dan finally spoke. "You were amazing back there. I was ready to support any decision you chose to make, but I think you did the right thing."

"What?" I asked. "I feel like I've let Uche down. How do I explain this to Vicky?"

Dan shook his head. "If this had gone to court, it would have been messier. You just rescued a couple's life inside there. Without this baby, the magnitude of their loss could have given any of them a stroke. They are nice people and will give Uche the very best, which I know you want for him."

"How will I cope?" I asked, staring into space.

Victory was sitting outside Mama Tunde's veranda when we entered the compound. She ran to embrace me. I couldn't share her enthusiasm. Dan carried her as we proceeded up the stairs.

As I bathed and fed Uche that night, his every smile and giggle drove shards of pain into my heart. His innocence was my redemption. As Victory played with him, it was evident how much they enjoyed being around each other. I was ending a good thing.

The next day, after dropping off Victory at school, I packed Uche's things in a small bag and took him to his new home. As I handed him over to Mrs. Tikolo, he let out a loud cry that made me wince. His crying voice trailed my exit as I battled with the pain gnawing at my heart.

Upon returning from school and finding an empty cot, my daughter asked the question I had come to dread. "Where is Baby?"

It had been two days since. A huge part of our lives was missing. The loss was palpable. I fiddled with my phone for some time and decided to call Dan. I had not heard from him in two days, which was unusual. He picked the call on the third ring. "Stella. How are you doing?"

"I feel terrible, Dan. Terrible. I wake up many times in the night thinking I heard his cry. His empty cot haunts me. I really need to see you."

"Stella, there is something I need to tell you," Dan said, his tone sounding distant.

"What is wrong?" I asked.

"Stella, I don't know how to say this. But I am no longer allowed to visit you."

"What?"

"See, Bola and I had a heated argument on Sunday night and it was about you. She asked me to choose between you and her."

"Ahn ahn! Which one be choose, again? Me and you dey do anything?"

"She said I give you too much attention, and that I visit you often. And that our relationship is suffering because of that. After some soul-searching, I realized she was right. I have a beautiful thing going on and I was throwing it all away."

His worries left me perplexed. Have I suddenly become a stumbling block?

"So, you chose?"

"Yes."

"You chose to stay away?"

He was silent.

I hung up, just before the tears escaped.

My loss had doubled.

FORTY-FIVE

The days that followed brought with them glimmers of hope. I buried myself in work, taking out my revenge on the sewing machine. Amazing designs emerged, my fury finding its usefulness.

Victory started eating more after I took her to visit Uche. The Tikolos hired a nanny to look after him. He looked well-fed and giggled with joy when he saw Victory. I carried him as much as I could and gauged him with my eyes. He looked healthy and happy and could stand with support. He was attempting to walk, landing on his bum after some few steps. Victory played with him, making him crawl all over the living room. When it was time to leave, the crying from both children ensued.

I was busy in my shop one afternoon when a black Toyota Corolla car parked just close to the entrance. Who could be blocking my door? The driver's door opened to reveal the person inside. I felt mixed emotions as Dan entered the shop. He responded to Ebele and Ola's greetings and sat in a corner.

"You got a new car?" I asked, breaking the silence.

"Yes," he said, forcing a smile.

"That's good. Congratulations."

I focused on the satin dress before me, avoiding his gaze.

"Stella."

"Yes?" I looked up, unable to hide the irritation in my voice.

"I came to know how you are doing and to tell you about the car. You have always encouraged me to save money and get one."

I was unmoved. "As you can see, I am fine. I will always be." Standing from the machine, I went to my work table to cut a piece of material.

"How are Victory and Uche?" Dan asked.

"They are doing great. Vicky asks about you sometimes."

His face lit up. Then, as though my comment had reminded him of something, he went to his car and returned with a red polythene bag.

"I got her this." He handed me the bag.

Inside it was a small golden-yellow dress, with patterned laces at the hem and beaded designs.

"Wow! She will love this. It is beautiful. Thank you." I put the dress away.

"Stella, there is something else."

I looked at him and noticed he was clutching something. He approached where I sat and placed it on the table. It was a small, hand-crafted invitation card.

"My wedding…is coming up next month. Both the traditional and white wedding are happening on the same day."

"Congratulations," I said, trying to smile. I could not. "How is Bola?"

"She is fine. We've been very busy, you know, with the wedding arrangements."

After some minutes, he stood up to leave. I accompanied him to his car.

"I am happy for you," I said, as he entered his car. "I may not show it, but I truly am."

"I know." He started the engine. "Stay happy."

As he drove off, I allowed the first tear to drop.

FORTY-SIX

"Stella, when are you calling us?"

For a moment, I wondered what she meant. "Calling you for what, Mama?"

"Your wedding, of course."

The seriousness in my mother's voice was unmistakable. This was no joke. I let out a laugh on my end of the line. "So, you want me to go to the street, catch a man, tie his neck with a rope and bring him to you, abi?"

It was her turn to laugh.

"Mama, I don't know what you want again o! I have given you a grandchild."

"Out of wedlock?" That was a low blow, even for her.

The ensuing silence was interrupted by a small cough at her end. "Stella *nwa m*, I didn't mean to insult or offend you. But you are not getting any younger. The Bible said that it is not good for a woman to be alone…"

I cut in. "That's not what the Bible said. It said 'man' not 'woman'."

"Are they not the same thing? What I mean is that marriage will make you more respected."

"Really? Mama, some men are devils o! They will just cut your life short."

The memories came flooding back. Jide almost ruined my life. If I was married to him and he was still alive, maybe I would have been dead. If only Mama knew.

But she was partly right. The loneliness was depressing. Seeing happy couples holding hands and seeming so much in love worsened the pain. I had begun to ask myself a series of questions. Was I not equally entitled to happiness? Was it a crime to wish to be loved? What was wrong with me?

My love adventure had been bitter-sweet - plenty of gall with some sprinkles of sugar. Prior to Jide, I had never housed a man all my life. So, why did I let him in? Why was I so serenaded by his charm that I let go of common sense?

He came, he saw and he destroyed. The pain and hurt of the moment could not equate with the brief stints of pleasure with him. Dan, the only sweetness I knew, was getting married. The completeness I felt whenever he was around was enough proof that I needed a man. Victory deserved a father figure in her life.

I had two major challenges, though. My daughter was my daughter was at a critical period of her development. She needed every bit of parental attention she could get. She was that silver lining in my cloud, my wellspring of hope.

My HIV status posed a second but bigger challenge. Mama had no idea how complicated my situation was; considering my status, getting into a relationship would require a very understanding and enlightened partner.

Still mulling over it, I dialled Nkechi. "Mama is mounting unnecessary pressure on me o!" I said, as soon as she picked.

She started laughing.

"You think it is funny, abi?"

"No oh!" She was still laughing. "Whenever she starts her marriage preaching, I remind her that you are the elder sister and that you ought to get married first."

"Oh! So na you dey cause all this *wahala*?" I felt like giving her a knock on the head.

"But come o! Why are you not searching sef? Eh? You don't go out. Fine babe like you. Every time you dey carry baby up and down."

I did not know whether to take her statement as an insult or mere talk. "How can I go out when I have Vicky to take care of? You know I can't bring a man to the house."

"OK. See the deal. I will come over and stay with you to help look after Vicky. You will start dating again. Agreed?"

I paused for a moment. I had mixed feelings about dating.

"You are not even serious." She gave a long hiss.

"Ok. Agreed," I said, after some hesitation. "Thank you."

True to her word, she came over with her bags the next day and the first thing she noticed was the empty cot. "How is Uche doing?"

"Very fine. He has started walking, small, small."

"Ehen?" she clapped her hands in amazement.

It was 5pm and so I moved to the sitting room to turn on the TV. "I made some yam porridge, there is also beef sauce and some rice if you prefer that."

"Oh okay,' she beamed and then she went to dish some for herself.

Moments later, she brought up the topic. "So, about this dating thing, what's your game plan?"

"Game plan, *kwa*?" I asked, surprised. My dating game was obsolete.

"You need a plan, a formidable one." She thought for a moment. "You need to start making yourself visible in circles where you can meet men. Weddings, ceremonies, church. Which group do you belong to in church?"

"None."

"The church is a place where you can meet good, God-fearing men. Do you still sing?"

"Only to myself," I said, shrugging.

I was the lead chorister in our village choir many years back, but I had not continued with my singing after arriving in Lagos.

"You should join the choir. But first, we need to change your hair. In fact, you need a total makeover."

"Na your department o! Abeg, do am free of charge."

She burst into laughter.

The next day, thanks to Nkechi's makeover skills, I was transformed. My hair had curly dark extensions that covered a part of my glistening face. I felt the stares from men trailing me as I passed them on the road and my self-esteem climbed new heights.

That evening, I went for choir practice at our church. The choristers were happy to welcome a new member into their ranks. I sat with the sopranos in front and sang away. The choir master, a tall, well-built fellow, kept looking in my direction. He was talented and could sing all the parts.

Towards the end of the practice, he asked me to introduce myself. I did and they welcomed me with a song. Despite feeling shy from all the attention, I was happy. It felt like I had found a new family.

As I made to leave after the practice, the choirmaster walked up to me. "You have an amazing voice."

His compliment was soothing.

"Thank you," I responded. "And you are so talented."

He smiled. "I am Akinola. Everyone calls me AK."

"Like the weapon?" I asked, laughing.

He pointed his index finger to the sky. "Only for Jesus."

"I like that."

His laughter was pleasant. As he walked me home, our discussion veered from personal details to preferred songs.

We became very good friends. He was in his mid-thirties and was admired by all the young girls in the church. A good number joined the choir just to get his attention. As we grew closer, he invited me to his house. I refused, citing many excuses.

One Sunday afternoon, after much prodding from Nkechi, I obliged. He lived in a one-bedroom apartment, with sparse but impressive furnishing. There were murals on the walls with framed paintings. A keyboard was on a stand at one end of the room.

"Your place is nice," I said. "You've got an exquisite taste."

"Thanks," he said, smiling. "Finally, you are here."

"Finally?" I asked, laughing.

He grinned. "Ehen nau! Make yourself comfortable." He disappeared into the kitchen and I went over to the piano and ran my fingers over the keys, loving the sound that filled the room.

Minutes later, I felt someone hold me from behind. Strange.

"Stella." It was his voice. There was something eerie about the way he sounded. I struggled to break free and moved towards the bed.

"What is wrong with you?" I asked, furious. "I just got here."

He looked remorseful and apologized before he offered me some drinks. I refused.

"Stella, why nau?" He looked hurt.

"I am fasting," I said. A convenient lie.

"Oh." He changed the topic. It was a monologue about everything from the murals on his wall to the weather outside.

Halfway into our conversation, he edged closer to where I was sitting.

"You wan start again, abi?" I said, but it was too late.

In an instant, he grabbed me like a possessed animal. We struggled as he rolled me over, his hands pinning my arms to the bed.

"AK, what is this madness?" I said, exasperated. "I will shout o!"

"No one will hear you. The door is sound-proof." He sounded determined and my heart began to race.

My alarm bells went off as I felt his left leg pushing apart my thighs. He had managed to lift my skirt.

"AK, stop! I beg you in the name of God."

He laughed. His turgid bulge was pressing against my crotch.

"AK, I am HIV positive. Please stop!"

"Na lie." His voice was cold.

It was ironic that the truth was not enough to set me free. I knew I had to change my tactics, so I let my body go limp under him. "Ok. Relax. I agree. We will do it. But let us go slow, please."

I kissed his lips to reassure him. He smiled and released my arms. I caressed his head.

"Do you have protection?" I asked, smiling.

He responded with a wink. "Let me bring it. I will be back shortly."

"Take your time," I said. "I want to undress."

He rose and went into the bathroom.

Without hesitation, I jumped up from the bed, grabbed my purse and ran. As I bounded down the stairs, I heard him shouting my name.

In a moment, I was on the street. I ran barefoot on the tarred road, my pace fuelled by a strange feeling that he was right behind me, inching closer. I could still hear his cold voice and feel his breath in my ears. I increased my pace, racing as though I was escaping from the devil.

Out of breath, I stopped at a kiosk - doubled over, panting, vaguely aware of everyone on the street staring at me. I stopped a motorcycle and reeled off the directions to my house.

The search for love was over.

FORTY-SEVEN

I banged on my door. Nkechi opened the door, alarmed. I rushed into the living room, bolting the door behind me.

"Stella, wetin happen?" she asked, as she followed me.

I walked straight into the bedroom. Victory was sleeping on the bed. I stood in front of the mirror and sighed. My lipstick was gone and my hair, disheveled. I closed my eyes in a bid to shut out the memories of that afternoon.

Nkechi's voice startled me. "Stella, what is wrong?" She was standing at the door, arms akimbo, with a worried look on her face. I tried to find my voice but it was the tears that came first. She hurried over and hugged me, urging me to talk.

I sobbed on her shoulders. "AK is a bloody rapist!"

"What?" Nkechi pulled away, shaking her head in disbelief.

"He almost raped me today. I was lucky to have escaped."

By the time I had finished narrating what transpired, she was fuming.

"You should have grabbed his testicles with your hands and crushed them. Bloody idiot!"

I sank into the bed, lost in thoughts. "The way he went about it, he must have done this to many unsuspecting girls before."

"Then why are no girls coming forward to make reports? Eh? Why is he still leading the choir every Sunday with a heart like the Devil's?" she asked, looking at me.

"Fear," I said. "Fear and shame. His victims would be too afraid and too ashamed to come forward. As he held me down, I felt so powerless. It doesn't help that our society sees the rape victim as weak. As though she brought it upon herself. Yet, her only 'crime' was to trust an animal. Most rapists are people we trust. Boyfriends. Uncles. Fathers. Some stranger we helped. And to think this was someone I was already falling in love with…"

My eyes were moist again. Nkechi hugged me.

"Nkay, I am tired," I said, amidst tears. "I am tired of loving and getting my heart broken. I am tired of men and their *wahala*."

"Babe, don't worry, *inugo*? Don't allow your bad experiences discourage you from loving again. God will send you a good man, the man of your dreams."

"When?" I asked her. "When I am old, with grey hairs?"

She smiled. "Obviously not! You will meet your man soon. Very soon."

I tried to smile.

She changed the topic. "You said Dan's wedding is on Saturday. Will you be going?"

"I have not made up my mind yet."

Nkechi looked at me, her head angled in the manner she kept it whenever she wanted to ask difficult questions. "Do you still have feelings for him?"

"I think so," I said, looking away.

Victory stirred in her sleep. "But it does not matter anymore." I added. "He will be getting married in six days."

"Did you let him know of your feelings for him?" Nkechi asked.

"There was no need. He already had a girl he was planning to marry. I even encouraged him to go ahead with the engagement."

"What? You mean you literally pushed your man into the arms of another woman? Eh? Now, he is about to marry her and here you are, roasting in your feelings. Babe, you don fall my hand finish." She gave a prolonged hiss.

"It was not exactly like that. He was already dating Bola before we reunited. And there were other issues…" I stopped myself.

"Whatever!" she dismissed my excuses with a wave of the hand. "It is not compulsory to go for the wedding. If you don't feel up to it, don't go."

I sighed. "Dan has been a wonderful friend. He came to invite me in person. I think I owe it to him to attend."

My phone rang. When I saw the name of the person calling, my heart skipped a beat. I gazed at the screen for some time, trying to decide whether to pick the call or not. The ringing stopped. Seconds later, it started ringing again.

"Who is it?" Nkechi asked.

"Bola. Dan's fiancée."

"Why is she calling you?"

"There is only one way to find out." I picked the call.

"Hello, Stella. How are you?" Bola's voice was crisp over the phone.

I frowned as I sensed anxiety in her voice.

"Good." I was in no mood for chit chat.

"I was calling to know if Dan slept over at your place."

I didn't know what to make of the question. I sat up straight and swallowed hard.

"No. He has not visited me in weeks. Why are you asking?"

I heard Bola sigh at her end. "He didn't come home yesterday," she replied, her words coming fast. I could hear her steady footfalls, as though she was pacing. "And his line has not been going through. He was on call at the hospital on Friday night and one of his colleagues saw him leave for home on Saturday morning. I have not seen him since and we had many places to go to yesterday…"

"Have you called Old Major? Maybe he went home to see his father." I scratched my head in deep thought.

"He was the first person I called. He said he has not seen him. He even said Dan promised to come by the family house later that evening but never showed up."

"That is quite unlike Dan. He usually calls if there is any change of plans…"

"Do you know anywhere else he might be? Old friends? Colleagues?"

I thought hard. No one came to mind. "No."

She gave another deflated sigh.

"Bola, Dan is a responsible man," I said. "I am sure he will come back home."

"Okay, okay. Bye." There was a click from her end as the line went dead.

"What was that about?" Nkechi asked. Victory had opened her eyes and pushed her right thumb into her mouth, sucking it. I gave her a soft slap on the back and she removed it, making a crying face. I stroked her braids with my left hand and scrolled through my phone's address book for Dan's number, then dialed it. *The number you are calling is not reachable at the moment.*

"It's Dan." I said to my sister. "He didn't return home yesterday. His line is not reachable. He is not at his father's. She was calling to know if he was here."

Nkechi shook her head. "Men!" she said. "Maybe he went somewhere to clear his head. You know wedding preparations can be so stressful. Or maybe he went to have 'the last supper' with any of his girlfriends." She added with a mischievous smile.

"Dan is not like that, joor! If he had any girlfriend, it would be me," I said, rolling my eyes.

Nkechi rocked back and forth in laughter.

"Little wonder Bola called you. Madam girlfriend!"

I glared at her in feigned annoyance.

For the next one hour, I sat on the bed, dialing Dan's number. Same response. *Not reachable.* I rose and went to the kitchen to prepare lunch, taking my phone with me. As I set Victory's food on the dining table, I dialed the number again. It rang.

"Nkechi, it is ringing!" I shouted.

Nkechi ran into the living room, Victory in tow. I listened with bated breath as it continued ringing. At the end, it stopped. No one picked. I dialed again and put the phone on loudspeaker. It rang and rang. No one picked. I dialed for the third time and was shocked. The line has been switched off. I dialed again. Same response. *Switched off.*

"Something is wrong," I said.

"Maybe someone stole his phone," Nkechi suggested.

"What if something has happened to him? What if he had an accident?"

I paced the room, trying to rid myself of the negative 'what if' scenarios playing out in my head.

I called Bola to inform her of the recent development.

We agreed to meet at Old Major's place in an hour.

FORTY-EIGHT

I took the longer route to Old Major's house, going through Lagos State University Teaching Hospital, where Dan worked. I searched the road for any car wreckage and scrutinized any black Toyota Corolla I saw. I asked the bus driver if he knew of any accident that had happened on that road.

He shook his head and gave me a strange look.

At the gate, Abdul noticed my worried expression.

"Have you seen Dan?" I asked him, as he opened the gate.

"No, Ma," he replied. "Worry don nearly finish Oga Major. *Walahi!*"

Bola was seated in the living room when I entered. Old Major was on the long sofa and he gave a weak smile when he saw me.

"Bola said you told her the phone rang." He sounded worried.

I hugged him and sat beside him.

"Papa, relax," I said. "Dan will come home. Maybe his phone was stolen."

I chatted with Bola about the wedding preparations. She reeled off all that had been done. Reception venue was secured, wedding gown and bridal train dresses were sorted, food and drinks were paid for. Everything was going according to plan.

I took the opportunity to ask Old Major about Dan's mother.

"Ah, Olamma." He closed his eyes for a moment, scratching his head. "She was the most beautiful woman I knew. We got married two months before the war broke out. She was a good woman, very good woman."

He continued. "But she usually had these terrible mood swings. At some points, she would withdraw, losing interest in everything. Sometimes, she would lash out at me in anger. I understood it was her mood. Most of the time, however, she was kind and very caring. She had a brilliant sense of humor. Some people said she was possessed by the *Ogbanje* spirit. I never believed any of those rubbish stories.

One day, I think Dan was five years old at that time, I came back from the shop and saw the whole house locked. My children were outside on the verandah, still in their school uniforms. They had not seen their mother.

I opened the door to behold the shock of my life. Olamma's body was hanging lifeless from the ceiling fan. On the table was a piece of paper with one word on it. *Goodbye*. Till today, I cannot understand why she did it."

The room was silent. We listened to the chiming of the clock, our anxiety rising with each passing minute. We waited for our phones to ring. No calls came. We listened for the swinging of the gates and Dan's car driving in. We heard nothing. I dialed Dan's number from time to time. It was still switched off.

Around 10pm, my phone rang. Everyone sat up. I looked at the screen and gave a disappointed sigh. It was Nkechi, calling to ask me if Dan had returned and if I was coming back that night. I answered in the negative.

By midnight, we were pacing the living room. Our anxiety had given way to worry. Our worries had matured into fear. Our brains confirmed what our hearts had been struggling to accept.

Dan was missing.

FORTY-NINE

We paced the living room of Dan's family house till dawn. As the light of the new day filtered in through the windows, we knew we had to do the needful. We clambered into Old Major's red Volvo, and headed for the nearest Police Station.

The policemen on the night shift were still milling around the expansive building when we arrived. We jumped out of the car as soon as Old Major killed the engine and the policeman at the gate eyed us with suspicion.

"Yes? Wetin happen?" His left hand reached for his rifle, lying on top a stack of old cement bags filled with sand.

"My son is missing," Old Major said.

"Oh." he said, still glaring at us. Seeming satisfied, he allowed us inside, pointing towards the main hall.

The main hall had a wooden counter by the side and some desks at one end. On the wall, there was a large white board detailing the names of the inhabitants of the various cells and the names of the police officers handling their cases. I scrolled down the list for Dan's name. No luck. The windows were still closed and the room was stuffy. Beads of perspiration formed on my forehead.

A stern-looking constable was at the central desk, with a chewing stick in his mouth. On sighting our approach, he put it away and straightened his shirt.

"What can I do for you?"

"We came to report a missing person," Old Major said.

The constable's eyes widened. "Who is this person and how long has he or she been missing?"

Old Major brought out a handkerchief from his pocket and mopped his brow. "The missing person is my son, Dr. Daniel Olisa. He was last seen leaving his place of work, Lagos State University Teaching Hospital, Ikeja, on Saturday morning - two days ago. He told his work colleagues he was going home."

Old Major placed his hand on Bola's shoulder. "His fiancée, here, said he never came home. We haven't gotten any calls as to his whereabouts since then. His cell phone rang for a moment and has been switched off since then."

The constable let out a yawn. "Was he driving?"

"Yes. A black Toyota Corolla which he bought a month ago," Old Major said.

The constable opened the top drawer in his desk and brought out some papers. "Fill this report. We will commence investigations immediately. It could be one of three things. First, that he was involved in an accident." I winced at the thought.

"He could also have been kidnapped," he added, facing me.

Old Major stared at the constable, his face contorted in anguish.

"Third, he may have made an urgent, emergency journey somewhere."

I prayed that the third scenario would be the case, despite the seeming unlikelihood.

"Was he under any kind of pressure lately?" the constable asked. "Any strange behaviour?"

We looked at one another and shook our heads. I could not recall Dan behaving in any strange way.

"His wedding is in five days' time, though," Old Major added.

"Arghhh! Very bad timing. Kai!" The constable glanced at Bola. She was fidgeting where she stood, a confused look on her face. "We will try and bring your groom back, okay?"

She nodded.

He told us we had to wait for the District Police Officer. We sat on a wooden bench adjacent to the wall. Chiemeka, Dan's elder sister, called to ask where we were. Bola called her colleague at work to tell her she would not be coming in that morning.

Just then, there was commotion from inside the cells. A young man was shouting.

"I am a Barrister, godammit! You are a very wicked man! You made me sleep over in a Police cell. I will show you!" He was pointing his index finger at a Police Officer who was escorting him out.

"Barrister, you are not above the law. And you no fit do me anything," the officer fired back. "If no be for this man wey just come bail you, I for make sure say you spend another night in the cell."

"What impudence! What effrontery!" The Barrister was spoiling for a fight, but the officer scoffed at him.

"You no go respect yourself abi? Yeye man! Person send you to collect rent, you collect the money, chop am. Come dey lie on top. You no dey shame?"

"Ladipo!" The constable called the officer to order and then asked him to go inside. He obeyed.

The Barrister murmured something about insolent bastards and left the station with the person who had come to bail him out.

Some minutes later, a police patrol Hilux pulled into the compound, causing a flurry of movement outside. I sat up. Two hefty police officers entered the door, dragging in with them three young men and a lady, all in handcuffs. One of the young men was bleeding from a thigh wound. The officer in the rear pushed him along as he struggled to move with difficulty. The lady was dressed in an orange singlet and combat shorts. Her face was devoid of any emotion.

The constable sat up. "Armed robbers," one of the officers said. "They were robbing two buildings on Jagaban Street. We were on patrol when we got the call. They even had the guts to engage us in a gun-fight," he added with a sneer.

"And the lady?" the constable asked, sizing her up.

"Na she be their leader o! You need to see her barking orders. We shot one of them dead. This one was lucky the bullet hit only his thigh. E for pierce your skull. Idiot!" The policeman struck the limping man with the butt of his gun. The young man yelled. There was a trail of blood from the door to the point where the injured man was standing and whimpering in pain.

"Oya, take them inside for questioning. After, lock them up in the cells. Idiots! Na for this cashless economy na im una dey go rob abi? Devil don catch una!" the constable bellowed as the robbery suspects were pushed into an inner room.

The DPO arrived some minutes after 8am. He strode into the room and went straight to his office. The constable followed him into the office. He emerged twenty minutes later and motioned us to follow him. Inside the office, an old, creaky air-conditioning unit was circulating cold air. The DPO asked us to sit.

"I have just been briefed on your case," the DPO said. "We have three theories: kidnap, accident, or travel. I will assign a detective to your case and will like you to cooperate closely with him. If it is a kidnap, the kidnappers will soon make contact. Inform us as soon as they do so. We will also check the surrounding hospitals and morgues, just in case. If Daniel had traveled, he will surely return." He turned to the constable. "Assign the case to Sergeant Okoli. Tell him I need results as soon as possible."

We thanked him and went to meet the Sergeant who was just assigned the case. A jovial officer, probably in his mid-thirties, his eyes narrowed in thought as we narrated the events again. He had already been briefed about Dan's situation by the constable but insisted on hearing it again, to see if there were more details to be gleaned.

"We will start by searching the emergency rooms of every hospital in Ikeja and every morgue," he said, after we had explained everything. The determination in his voice offered some comfort. "If this is a kidnap, they will make contact, soon. Alert us immediately."

We met Chiemcka at the main desk on our way out. Old Major brought her up to speed on the progress made.

As we exited the station, I took a casual glance at the police Hilux parked in the middle of the yard and froze in horror. Sprawled in the trunk was the bloodied corpse of a young man. The soles of his feet were pale and his face was swollen and disfigured. Some flies hovered around the corpse. Lying beside him were some machine guns with bullets scattered in the trunk, most soaked in his blood. I felt chills sweep through me and looked away.

A young life, wasted.

FIFTY

"No, no, that is not him," I said. We were at the morgue and I was asked to identify Dan among unclaimed bodies. We've been searching for four days. I tried hard to suppress the flood of nausea welling up, swallowing the excess saliva that had pooled in my mouth. The pungent smell of the embalming fluid made me feel woozy. My eyes stung, the formed tears blurring my vision. I wiped them away with the back of my hand.

The mortician, a bald, short, good-natured man, noticing my discomfort, headed for the door. "I am sorry, that is all we've got."

I nodded and took one last sweeping look at the room. It was more spacious than the others but also poorly lit and crammed full of dead bodies. The fortunate ones lay naked on the slabs, while the rest lay on the floor. The smell of the embalming fluid hung in the air like a thick curtain and I was happy to leave that grim place. The silence was broken only by our departing footsteps.

A gust of fresh air hit my nostrils as we emerged outside. I took a lungful and tried to dispel the images of the countless, naked bodies I just saw.

"Any luck?" Sergeant Okoli asked. He was seated on a wooden bench in front of the morgue, the third one we had visited that day.

I shook my head.

The mortician cleared his throat. Jolted by his subtle reminder, I opened my purse and handed him a crisp five hundred naira note. "Thank you very much."

He beamed. "No problem, Ma. I pray that you find him alive."

I nodded in agreement, trying to force a smile as Sergeant Okoli rose from the bench and headed to the parked police van we had come in.

My steps slowed as my phone rang. It was Old Major.

"Good evening, Papa. Any news?"

"Stella nwa m. We have searched all the hospitals in Amuwo-Odofin and Festac area. We also searched the morgues. Nothing." His voice was laden with grief.

"We will keep looking, Papa. Just stay strong. We will find him. How is Bola holding up?"

"Ahhh! She has been crying all day. The wedding is supposed to be held tomorrow, you know. We are driving back to the house. I think I have seen enough hospitals and dead bodies for one day."

"OK. I will come over to the house."

I climbed into the front seat of the Police van. The Sergeant was already seated behind the wheel, patiently waiting.

"Thanks a lot for today," I said.

He shrugged. "I was just doing my duty."

As the police van approached the hospital gate, Sergeant Okoli fumbled in his breast pocket and brought out a tally which he returned to the grinning security man.

The car turned onto the road and soon joined the long line of other cars moving very slowly.

"Kai! Traffic. Where are you headed?" he asked.

"I am going to Amuwo-Odofin but I will make a stop at Egbeda to check on my daughter. This traffic is gradually building up."

"Yeah. It is almost 5pm. Evening rush, some will not get home till 10pm."

I sighed. "That's Lagos for you. Which side do you stay at?"

"Festac. 5th Avenue. How are you related to the missing person, Dan?"

I scratched my head. "Well…we used to date."

"Oh. I see."

We drove in silence for some time. I dialed Dan's number one more time. It was still switched off.

"His wedding is tomorrow, right?"

"Yes."

He chuckled. "It seems someone does not want this wedding to happen."

It struck me what he might be thinking. "No, Officer. Dan has been a great friend and I would never wish him harm."

"Who said anything about harm?" He pulled the car over. "Let me make something clear to you, Stella. I have watched you closely since this investigation began. The fact that you are so motivated to find Dan could mean one of two things. You may genuinely want him back. Or you may be covering your tracks. I would love to believe the former. But make no mistake, until we get any important leads in this case, I have my eyes on you."

I felt my legs weaken. His last statement broke my heart. "Just take me home."

I looked out of the window as he drove, my chest tightening with pain.

We entered my street and the van stopped in front of my house. I came down, slamming the car door behind me.

"Should I wait for you?" he asked.

"Don't!"

I hurried into my compound and ran up the stairs.

"Mummy!" Victory welcomed me with a warm embrace as soon as Nkechi opened the door. I hugged her little frame and carried her up in the air. She yelled in excitement.

"I missed you, Vicky darling. Have you eaten?"

She nodded, smiling.

"Any progress? Is he back?" Nkechi asked.

I shook my head. "And tomorrow is the wedding."

"There will be no wedding. Except a miracle happens."

"I will be going over to Old Major's place. I just came to check on you and Vicky. Thanks for everything."

Nkechi nudged me towards the bathroom. "Oya, go and change those clothes. And eat something."

I set Victory down on the bed and went into the bathroom.

FIFTY-ONE

The look on Abdul's face when I arrived at Dan's family house, told me nothing had changed. I noticed the police van parked beside the red Volvo.

The living room was full. Sergeant Okoli was seated with Old Major on one sofa. Dan's two sisters, Chiemeka and Añuli were in the room. Añuli held Bola, who was whimpering in a corner. Chiemeka was discussing with her husband, Mike, a pastor. I greeted them as I entered, dropped my phone on the centre table and sat in a corner.

The Sergeant rose to leave. "Like I said earlier, keep all lines open and notify me if you get any calls," he instructed, then bade everyone goodnight. Old Major saw him off to the door.

We sat in silence, all eyes fixed on the centre table. Six phones were laid out, close to each other. None rang. "Chai! I am finished!" Bola exclaimed, ushering a fresh round of tears. I went over to console her.

"Babe, he will return. You hear?"

"When?" she asked, looking at me.

I swallowed hard.

"How do I tell all the invited guests that there will be no wedding?" she asked no one in particular, tears running down her cheeks.

"Of course, there will be a wedding," Mike said, rising to his feet. "God is about to do a big miracle." He lifted his bible and broke into a worship song. We all joined in.

We prayed all night. As the cock crows signalled the dawn of a new day, our weary eyelids were heavy with sleep. Our sore voices chorused the last rounds of the 'Amen'. I sank onto the sofa, exhausted, and slept off.

I dreamt of Dan, dressed in a well-tailored black suit, rousing me from sleep. I opened my eyes. It was Chiemeka, offering me a steaming plate of rice.

"What is the time?" I asked, setting the plate down on a stool.

"8.30am," she said.

Bola and Añuli were up, staring at their plates of food with disinterest. Old Major was still sleeping. Pastor Mike was gone.

The aroma of the jollof rice triggered more rumblings in my stomach. We had not eaten dinner the previous night, and had spent a great deal of energy disturbing heaven. I took two spoonfuls. It tasted good. Old Major roused from his sleep, opened his eyes, looked at the clock and shook his head.

"Good morning, Papa," we chorused. He nodded and entered his room.

We ate in silence, occasionally stealing glances at the wall clock and staring at the phones on the centre table. As soon as the clock struck 9.00am, Bola gave a loud cry. "There goes my wedding!"

I rushed to her side.

Just then, we heard a phone ring. The ringing phone was Old Major's. For an instant, we sat transfixed, eyes on the centre table, wondering if we heard right. It continued ringing. Old Major ran into the living room and picked it.

"Hello…Oh, Dan!" His face brightened up. "My son, where have you been? We have been looking for you…"

Bola snatched the phone from his ears. "Daniel!" she screamed. "Why did you do this to me?"

We saw her countenance change from anger to morbid fear. She pressed some buttons and dropped the phone on the centre table.

"Mr. Fabian Olisa, I have your son, Daniel." The baritone at the other end of the line was businesslike, devoid of any warmth.

"Now that you have confirmed that he is alive, listen very carefully and do exactly as I say. Otherwise, we will send him to you in pieces."

I rubbed my hands over my forearm to rid it of gooseflesh. We listened as he spoke, our faces contorted in worry. When he was done, the line went dead. I looked at Bola, the fresh tears on her face betraying the horror of the moment.

I hugged Old Major, rattled as he was by the call. I sought for words of consolation but found none. Instead, I felt my own dam of emotions break open.

The tears flowed, unhindered.

FIFTY-TWO

"Ten million naira! Where on earth will I get that amount of money?" Old Major said, his hands on his head. "Chai! I am finished."

For one moment, I wished it was one huge prank and that Dan was alive and well, safe, and acting his own part of a script. But Dan was not the type to play expensive pranks and the male voice on the other end of the line, certainly was not joking. He sounded very polished, but his meanness could be felt miles away despite his crisp English. This was really happening.

He had given three clear and concise instructions. *Get ten million naira before forty-eight hours. Send Bola to bring it to a later-to-be-disclosed location. Don't involve the Police.* We looked on, dazed, as he reeled out the instructions. In the background, we could hear Dan screaming.

"What are you doing to my son?" Old Major had asked.

"Nothing serious. Just some morning exercise."

What we heard sounded like someone was punching Dan. There was intermittent laughter. The man repeated his instructions and then the line went dead.

For some minutes, we looked at each other, speechless. The unfolding reality felt surreal.

"I have only two shops in Alaba. Even if I sell the shops with their contents and this house, I am not even sure of raising five million naira. And that will take at least a week." Old Major said, shaking his head.

"Papa, we will find a way," I said, holding his shoulders.

Bola sat in a corner, brooding. Chiemeka and Añuli were seated on the sofa, staring into space.

"Let's call the Police...that detective," Bola said.I shot her a glance, then looked at Old Major.

"What other options do we have, eh?" she continued, looking around the room. "How can we raise ten million in forty-eight hours?"

The room was silent. After a while, I spoke up. "But you heard the man clearly. Never involve the Police..."

"He was just bluffing," Bola said. "Which kidnapper will tell you to involve the police, eh? Don't the Police catch some of them and rescue their victims?"

I looked at Old Major again, wanting him to say something.

"I will call Sergeant Okoli," he said, picking up his phone from the centre table.

"Hello, Officer...Good morning. It was a kidnap...No, they contacted us...ten million in forty-eight hours...Okay. Please come quick, quick."

When the Sergeant arrived, he listened as Old Major narrated what had transpired, stopping occasionally to make some notes in a small, black notebook.

"What are we going to do?" Old Major asked him.

"We are going to play along," he said, looking around the room. "It is important we realize how crucial this is. If they get any whiff that you have involved the Police, then I am afraid for your son. There have been some recent kidnap cases and they sound like the same group."

"What about the money?" Old Major asked.

"Don't worry. I will take care of everything from here," Sergeant Okoli said.

He turned to Bola. "I will be back with a team of officers in the evening to prepare you, and walk you through the entire process."

The next morning, I met a small crowd in Dan's family house. I had gone home the previous evening to freshen up and drop instructions with my student tailors, having not been to the shop in a week.

"We have barely twenty-four hours left. You have to try your best to stay calm," Sergeant Okoli said to Bola.

Some plain-clothed policemen walked around the room while Chiemeka, Añuli, Mike and Old Major sat on the sofa.

"I can't do this," Bola said, sobbing.

"You can," Sergeant Okoli said, placing a hand on her shoulder. "Don't you want to see your hubby again, uh?"

She nodded, amidst sobs.

"Good. Let's go over the routine again," he said, and motioned to another officer who adjusted some wires on Bola's body.

"Remember, we will be hearing everything. And we will sweep in and remove you from the place at the slightest sign of danger. But you have to remain calm, OK?"

Bola nodded, still shaking.

They spent the whole evening rehearsing the routine till Bola mastered it. "I think we are done for the day," the Sergeant said, glancing at the clock. It was 9.45pm. "We will be back very early in the morning."

"Thank you very much, Officer," Old Major said, escorting them to the door.

We had no choice but to hope.

FIFTY-THREE

By 8.00am, the Sergeant and his team arrived, fully armed. Bola was dressed up, the wires hidden from plain sight. They went through the routine again.

"I am not entering there empty-handed, am I? These guys are expecting money," Bola said. There was panic in her voice.

"Don't worry," Sergeant Okoli said. "We have two bags in the van, containing some counterfeit money to the tune of that amount. There is no way they would know the difference on sight."

Bola nodded. She was wringing her hands as they went over the routine again.

At exactly 9.00am, Old Major's phone rang. The Sergeant motioned him to pick the call and place it on loud speaker mode.

"Hello, Sir...Good morning, Sir...I have your money..." Old Major began, his voice shaking.

The voice we heard next was stern. "Mr. Fabian Olisa, what was the third instruction I gave you?"

A gasp escaped Old Major's lips. "You said...never to involve the Police...Sir."

"And what have you done?" We heard a hiss on the other end. "Major, I have my eyes on you. An hour ago, three police vans entered your compound. You just killed your son. His blood is on your hands."

"No, please Sir, let me explain..."

The line went dead.

Old Major sank into a sofa, shaking in grief. Bola tore out all the wires under her blouse and gave a loud howl. Sergeant Okoli stood transfixed. I had my hands on my head, confused.

"I knew this was a bad idea," Bola said, sobbing.

"Shut up!" I bellowed, fuming. "You were the one that suggested we involve the police. Now, see."

The Sergeant glared at me and went outside to discuss with the other policemen.

"Daniel *nwanne m* o!" Añuli screamed, amidst tears. I moved over to console her.

"We are going back to re-strategize," Sergeant Okoli said, as he returned. "I believe we will come up with a way to rescue your son."

Three hours after the policemen left, Abdul entered the living room, carrying a small box wrapped in brown paper. "Oga, someone leave this for gate. The pesin knock, as I come outside, I no see anybody. Na only this thing I see. And e carry your name."

Old Major collected the parcel from him and set it on the centre table. The surface of the brown paper had the words 'To Mr. Fabian Olisa' handwritten on it. He looked around at the rest of us who were watching, our faces betraying our curiosity, before he proceeded to tear off the brown paper covering.

Underneath the paper was a small box, the kind that contained wrist watches. He opened it.

"Jesus Christ!" he shouted, squirming in disgust. We all drew back, our emotions caving in at once. Lying at the centre of the box was a human finger, the bloodied end representing where it was severed from the hand.

"Dan's ring finger!" Bola screamed, slumping to the ground. "They've cut Dan's ring finger!"

I took one more look at the bloody, severed digit and felt tears coursing down my cheeks.

Our hopes were melting like thin ice.

FIFTY-FOUR

The ringing phone on the centre table jolted us. Old Major picked it up, his hands trembling.

"Oga, why nau? Why did you cut my son's finger?"

Bola gestured to Old Major to put the phone on speaker mode. He did.

The voice at the other end laughed for some time. In the background, we heard someone, howling in pain. "I can see you got my gift," the voice began. "First, I am not your Oga. You can call me Shadow. Second, you forced my hand. Third, if you mess things up again, you can just go and buy a coffin."

There was silence in the living room as we listened.

"Mr. Fabian Olisa, besides having my eyes on you and your son for some time now, I know you. I knew that you could not come up with ten million naira even if I gave you a week. I just wanted to know how good you are at following instructions. As a Major in the defunct Biafran Army, I expected you to do better. But you failed." He took a deep pause.

Old Major's face cut a pathetic picture.

"Which brings me to the second set of instructions. I want to make this very simple and unite you with your son. Get the little sum of five million naira within forty-eight hours. Stella will bring the money to a location I will give you later…"

I froze as I heard my name. Everyone in the room turned to look at me. Trickles of hot fluid escaped me, soaking my underwear. The voice continued, "Oh, Stella. Don't be surprised. Dan and I had a little chat."

He broke into another round of laughter. The next moment, his voice was serious. "Don't even try to wear a wire like Bola."

Bola looked confused as I was. How the hell could he know that?

"The third instruction is the same as before. If you like, call that scumbag Sergeant Okoli and gamble away your son's life...or what is left of it." The line went dead.

My surprised stare was greeted by the confused look on everyone's face. Bola finally broke the silence. "How on earth does he know everything? He seems aware of our every move!" she said, throwing up her hands in despair.

Old Major sat down on the couch, resting his chin on his palms. "That boy...Shadow or whatever he calls himself, is very smart. How he got to know everything, I can't say. But one thing I know is that I am no longer involving the Police. He may have an insider among them."

He had just voiced what I was thinking. The thought that a dangerous stranger knew about me filled me with dread.

"So, how are we going to raise the money?" I asked, looking around the room. Everyone's eyes said the same thing. This would be hard.

We began brainstorming. Old Major placed some calls to some of his friends pleading with them to purchase his shops for two million naira each. They all turned him down. The best offer he got was for one million naira apiece. He had no choice.

"I have three hundred thousand naira in savings," I volunteered. "I can also sell my second shop for an additional two hundred thousand naira."

I saw tears form in Old Major's eyes at my words.

"You don't have to sell your shop," he said.

I held his arm. "Allow me to do all I can, please."

"I have two hundred thousand naira in savings," Bola said. "I could take a salary advance of hundred thousand naira, making it up to three hundred thousand." Old Major nodded in gratitude.

"I have a hundred thousand naira I kept aside for my rent," Añuli said. "I will get that."

"Where will you live?" Old Major asked her.

"I can come and live with you, Papa," she said, hugging him.

"I have a hundred thousand naira in savings," Chiemeka said. "I will talk to Mike to see if he could lend us some money from the church development funds."

"So, we have roughly three million naira," I said. "We are running out of time. Let us go and get the money and figure out how to get the balance."

"Please, we should all be very careful," Old Major said, as I rose to leave. "I no longer know who to trust."

I knocked on my door, sauntering in as soon as Nkechi opened it. I sank into a sofa.

"How did the rescue go?" she asked.

"How do you think it went?" I snapped back. "That devil knew our every move. He even sent us a souvenir. Dan's ring finger in a box." The mere thought of it churned my stomach.

"*Jesu!*" Nkechi had her hands on her head.

Just then, Victory appeared at the adjoining door, rubbing her eyes and yawning. Our voices must have woken her. I tried to muster a smile.

"Sweetheart," I said, beckoning her to come. I carried her on my lap, resting her head on my bosom. "How have you been my darling?"

"Fine." She was still sleepy. I stroked her hair, running my hand along the length of each braid.

"They asked us to bring five million in two days," I said, in a hushed tone.

"What?" Nkechi said.

Victory stirred. I gestured to Nkechi to keep her voice down.

"How will Old Major raise that?"

"He is selling his shops in Alaba. All of us are contributing money. I am selling my second shop."

Nkechi stared at me in disbelief. "Like seriously?"

I nodded. "It will fetch at least an extra two hundred thousand naira. We need every dime we can get."

"You suffered very much to get that shop," she said, rising to her feet.

She paced the room, lost in thought. "Don't sell the shop. I have two hundred and thirty thousand naira in the bank. I will lend you the money from there."

Her response lifted a heavy load off my chest. "Thank you so much. I will pay you back as soon as I can."

"Before nko?" she said. "I am just doing this for Dan, your divinely-ordained husband whom you donated to another woman."

"Stop it, sis! Thank you. Really. I appreciate you."

As I lay on the bed that night, my mind wandered to Dan. Here was an unproblematic, well-behaved young man, caught up in something we could not explain. Dan spent his working hours saving lives.

Yet, he has missed his wedding. He has lost his freedom. He has lost his finger. He is at the verge of losing his life if we do not raise five million naira in the next thirty-six hours.

Why do bad things happen to good people?

FIFTY-FIVE

The next morning, we were all gathered in Old Major's living room, counting cash. On the centre table were bundles of one thousand naira notes waiting to be counted. I mopped beads of sweat off my brow.

"How much now?" I asked Bola, tossing a bundle into a nearby Ghana-must-go bag.

"Two point eight million," she said, looking up from the big calculator she held in her hands. I looked at the remaining uncounted cash on the centre table and shook my head. We needed an urgent miracle.

After another hour of collective, furious cash-counting, the centre table surface was empty. We all turned to Bola to hear the final figure. She shook her head. "Four million. We are one million naira short."

Old Major's hands went up his head. "I have sold everything but this house. I even borrowed an extra one million naira. And it is still not enough."

For the next hour, we sat in silence thinking of where to raise the balance from.

"Chiemeka, you said you will talk to your husband about lending us some money from the church's development fund," I said.

"Oh, that," she said, looking away. "I spoke to him about it. He said he cannot approach the church for it."

"Why?" I asked, rising from the floor.

She shrugged. "He said if he told them he needed the money for a ransom, they would not oblige him.

And he cannot lie to the church council." I sighed, scratching my head.

Just then, an idea occurred to me. I had one last, painful turn to make.

"I need to go somewhere in search of the balance," I said, to no one in particular.

Old Major gave me a worried look.

"Don't worry. I will be fine," I said, exiting the living room.

I stopped before the big, black gate, unsure of whether to proceed. I did the sign of the cross and knocked. Moments later, the gateman appeared and gave a faint smile of recognition. I entered the compound.

Chief Tikolo had sighted me from the balcony of the duplex. "Stella, Stella. Long time no see."

I greeted him and proceeded into the living room. His wife was seated on the sofa, playing with Uche. She rose as soon as I entered.

"Ma-ma," Uche said. I was surprised he had not forgotten what he used to call me. I kissed him on both cheeks and hugged Mrs. Tikolo.

Chief Tikolo soon joined us. "I hope all is well, my daughter," he asked.

I shook my head. "I am in desperate need of help."

They listened as I narrated Dan's story to them. "The day I gave Uche to you, you gave me a cheque of one million naira which I turned down. I know it sounds foolish, but I really need that money now."

Chief stood up and left the room, without saying a word. I stared at the tiles on the floor, very certain that I had made a big fool of myself and appeared like a cheap extortionist. His wife also stood up and left the living room. My despair and embarrassment deepened.

This was a terrible idea, Stella. You should not have come.

Moments later the couple returned, their faces expressionless. I braced myself for the worst.

"Stella, you deserve more than this," Chief Tikolo said, handing me a cheque.

I stared at him in disbelief and then looked at the cheque. It was in my name. A million naira.

I jumped up in joy. "Thank you…thank you," I said, hugging them.

"Always come to us if you need anything," Mrs. Tikolo said.

As the gate closed behind me, I checked my watch. 3.40pm. I had twenty minutes before the banks closed. I flagged down a bike and asked him to take me to the nearest Zenith Bank branch.

"Madam, e far small o," he said. "Two-fifty naira."

I mounted his bike. "I will pay you double if you can get there before 4pm."

At exactly 4pm, I jumped down in front of the bank, flustered. I handed the bike man a five hundred naira note and ran inside. The security man at the automated door looked at me in pity and opened it for me. Panting, I joined the queue in the banking hall, my heart filled with relief.

My phone rang as I exited the bank, the withdrawn cash wrapped in a black polythene bag under my left arm. It was Old Major.

"Any luck?" he asked. The uncertainty in his tone was unmistakable.

"Papa, Dan is coming home tomorrow."

I heard him shout with joy and break into a song, a song of victory.

FIFTY-SIX

"Dan will be coming home tomorrow." Nkechi's eyes lit up at my words when she opened the door. On entering the living room, I put on the standing fan and turned it around to face me, relieved as the sweat on my face began to evaporate. The forceful draft of air was exhilarating.

Nkechi sat on the arm of the sofa, the smell of her cologne a pleasant change from the smell of sweat in the queue at the banking hall.

"They said they will release him tomorrow?" she asked.

"Not exactly. But we have the complete money and I will be taking it to them tomorrow."

I turned in time to note the shock on her face.

"You? Why must it be you? Why not his father or any of his sisters?"

I shook my head. "*Nne*, I don't know. His captor, Shadow, requested that I bring the ransom."

She gave a deflated sigh. "Any address yet?"

"No. He'd probably call at the last minute to give the location. That bastard. People just wake up and kidnap a young, hardworking doctor and then put his loved ones through untold suffering to raise an outrageous amount of money. Just to satisfy their greed? This is just pure evil."

Nkechi put her arm over my shoulder. "Don't worry. You will be fine. Tomorrow it will be all over."

"Where is Victory?" I asked, standing up.

"Oh. She is at Mama Tunde's house playing with the other children. Let me go and get her."

"Okay." I entered the room, exhausted.

The next morning, I kissed Victory goodbye just before leaving. I dressed her up earlier and packed her lunchbox.

"I will be back this evening, Sweetheart," I said as I lifted her up. Her beautiful eyes gazed into mine. "And Mummy will never go away again."

She nodded, her face breaking into a smile. I tickled her armpits as I set her down. "Be a good girl, okay?"

"Okay." The sound of her laughter filled the room.

Nkechi locked up after me as I left, Victory standing in the stairway, waving. I waved back.

Old Major was on the verandah when I arrived, clad in his well-worn blue *kaftan*. He had been wearing it since his son was kidnapped, ten days ago.

He smiled on seeing me. "*Nne,* welcome," he said, accompanying me into the living room.

Añuli was cleaning the centre table with a cloth. A broom lay by her side. She noted my hesitation and smiled. "You can sit. I just finished sweeping. *Nnoo.*"

"Has he called?" I asked Old Major, as soon as we were seated.

He shook his head and reached for his phone. He dropped it on the centre table. "Chiemeka! Bring the bag. Stella is here." He turned to me. "Bola just left for her office. She said they needed her for something urgent."

Chiemeka emerged from the room, carrying a blue, chequered Ghana-must-go bag. "This bag is heavy o!" she said, setting it down in a corner of the room. I opened the black polythene I came with, brought out the money I had withdrawn from the bank and put it into the bag. It was all inside there - five million naira worth of blood, sweat and tears.

"Do you know why they call it a 'Ghana-must-go' bag?" Old Major asked, looking at me. I shook my head, eager to hear the story and distract him from further worrying. Anything was better than thinking about what was to come.

"In January 1983, President Shagari ordered all immigrants without the right papers to leave the country within a few weeks. At that time, there were over two million illegal immigrants. A million of them were from Ghana."

"Why would he give such an order?" I asked.

"So many reasons were given. We don't know which to believe. Fuelled by rumours of possible maltreatment in Lagos after the February deadline, within few days of the announcement, two million people packed what they could into these chequered bags and thus began a massive exodus towards Seme border."

"That sounds unfair," Añuli said.

Old Major sighed. "Well, in 1969, Ghana expelled many immigrants, including Nigerians, under the Alien's Compliance Order…"

The sound of the ringing phone cut him short, and just like that, all our worries came rushing back. I glanced at the wall clock. 9.00am. Seeing Old Major's hands tremble as he picked the phone, I prayed the whole ordeal would be over soon, for his sake. He was an old man, and there was only so much stress his health could take.

We watched in trepidation as he put the phone on speaker mode. We heard a voice screaming in the background. A familiar male voice came on. "Mr. Fabian Olisa, do you have my money?"

"Yes, Yes…Sir. Five million. Complete," Old Major said.

"Good. Stella will bring the money to me on Owode road. It is off the Lagos-Badagry Expressway. She should come alone and stop in front of the high-tension electric poles there. Leave your phone with her. She should be there in two hours."

"Okay. But I need to know…that my son is safe," Old Major said, his voice shaking.

Shadow hissed. His next words were a reprimand.

"Keep wasting your time." The line went dead.

"So, we are just going to hand him five million without knowing whether my son is dead or alive?" Old Major said, pacing the room.

I held him. "Papa, don't worry. He is alive. Let's just do as he said. We are running out of time."

He shook his head. "Okay. I will drive you up to the Owode road and wait for you and Dan to come back."

Añuli carried the Ghana-must-go bag to the car and placed it on the back seat. I entered the front of the vehicle with Old Major. He turned to me, "We'll drive through Mosunmola and emerge at Ojo Road. We will then join the Expressway."

We drove in silence, my eyes going frequently to the wristwatch on my left wrist to check the time. The Volvo's engine roared at every intersection as Old Major switched the gears. I cleaned my sweaty palms on the denim I wore, upbraiding myself on how terrible I looked.

The denim was Nkechi's idea. I had donned a satin gown and was finishing my make-up when she entered my bedroom, staring at me in dismay.

"You can't go out dressed like that," she said, touching the material to demonstrate how light it was. "They can just tear this into pieces."

She had a point. I had not even considered any danger to myself.

"I am just going to drop money, not wine and dine with them," I said.

In response, she had gone to my wardrobe and fished out a long-abandoned pair of jean trousers.

I wore it only once in the previous year, preferring the allure of native fabrics, so I struggled to fit into it. It felt awkward buttoning it up.

"It fits you perfectly," Nkechi said, standing behind me in front of the mirror. "Good for moving around fast Also, all the curves in the right places. Dan will like it."

I pushed her away and found a black, cashmere blouse to go with the jeans. I made sure it was long enough to cover all the curves in question. Looking pretty was the last thing on my mind.

We drove for another hour, slowing down at the parts of the road undergoing construction. I watched the trees and vegetation on the side of the road receding fast as we made progress. A clearing with a small kiosk appeared in the distance. Old Major slowed down to ask for directions..

An unclad boy was rolling in the sand in front of the shop. He eyed us with suspicion as we approached and started crying. A man in a brown *danshiki* emerged from the kiosk and carried the boy up. He smiled at us, exposing his missing front row teeth.

"We are looking for the direction to Owode road," Old Major told him.

"Owode...Owode," he said, setting the boy down on a bench.

He nodded in sudden realization. "E no too far again. The next turn by your right. Just dri-i-ive." He pointed into the distance, stretching his last syllable.

We thanked him and left. We made the turn to Owode road and drove for some distance until we saw the metal frame of a high-tension electric pole ahead of us. The whole place looked deserted as not a single person was in sight. Old Major parked beside the road and killed the engine.

"What now?" I asked, trying to mask the fear that had gripped me.

"We wait for his call."

I clasped my palms together, trying to calm my nerves.

After ten minutes of breathing exercises, the phone rang. Old Major handed it to me.

"Hello," I said, closing my eyes.

"Stella." It was Dan's voice.

In an instant, I opened my eyes and sat up. "Dan! Are you alright?"

Shadow's voice came on. "Why you no dey at the high-tension with my money? Or do you want this man dead?"

"Sorry. Please. I am close. I was waiting for your call."

"You have five minutes." The line went dead.

I fumbled with the Volvo's handle, pushing it open. Grabbing the bag from the back seat, I broke into a run, dragging the bag along. In a few minutes, I was at the high-tension wires electric pole, panting.

There was no one in sight. On both sides of the road were lush vegetation and a few strange and short palm trees, different from the ones we had in my village.

There was rustling in the bush opposite me. Just then, I felt cold metal touch the back of my neck and shuddered.

"Turn around slowly and pass me the bag," a male voice said.

I turned to stare into the barrel of a pistol. The man holding the gun was light-skinned and well-dressed, with a rough beard.

I handed him the bag, trying not to look into his face.

"Turn around," he said.

I obeyed. "Where is Dan?" I asked, my eyes scanning the bush in front of me.

In that instant, I felt a jab on my neck. I swung around, knocking an object from his hand. It fell to the ground. An empty syringe.

The man had a smirk on his face. "Sorry."

For a moment I was confused, wondering what was going on. Then, it started - this woozy feeling. My body was going numb and my vision started to blur. The only thing on my mind was to escape with my life. I tried to run but my legs gave way under me.

Staggering to the other side of the road, I fell into the surrounding darkness.

FIFTY-SEVEN

I woke up with a throbbing headache. My eyelids stung as I opened them, a beam from a flashlight was moving from one eye to the other.

"Shadow, she don wake," a voice said.

I blinked in discomfort, the coldness of the bare cement floor on which I lay caused me to shiver. The person who had spoken walked away with the light. My fingers moved from my wet blouse to my soaked jean trousers, my teeth chattering from the cold.

I groped around in the darkness and my hand hit a metal bucket. The light flashed in my direction and continued to skirt around in the distance. Around me, the ground was wet. The light fell on the wall: unplastered, just blocks held with cement mortar. It fell on the floor again and approached my direction, accompanied by some footsteps.

"Bring her here." The deep, familiar voice was at the other end of the room.

The footsteps stopped close to me and a pair of strong hands grabbed my shoulders, forcing me to my feet. The person dragged me forward by the hand and I struggled to move, my legs feeling like jelly.

"Easy, Iron. She's a woman."

The dancing flashlight before us helped me make out a man in a seat. I fell on my knees as we stopped in front of him. My knees were hurting and I was more comfortable kneeling.

"Tell Lucky to bring the light," he said.

The man with the flashlight disappeared into the next room, leaving me and the seated man in darkness.

I recognized his voice. Shadow. I struggled with my dizziness. "You promised to release him when we bring the money. You promised!"

He laughed. "They say there's no honour among thieves. Do you believe that?"

He struck a match and, in that instant, I saw his pristine features as his eyes bore into mine. The savage who cut off Dan's finger, drugged and kidnapped me as I came to deliver his ransom, did not look like the brute I had imagined. The match died out and he let out a puff from the glowing cigarette in his mouth.

The second man returned, carrying a kerosene lamp. Another man walked in tow, carrying a rifle. The second man shifted some guns on the table to make space for the lamp. I noticed that a laptop computer was open on the table. A wire came in from one of the open windows to an extension box at the foot of the table. At another end of the room was a stack of mattresses and rolled-up mosquito nets.

"Ah, she is awake," the third man said, smiling. "And she is beautiful."

He ogled my wet frame and I folded my arms across my chest.

"Cut it out, Lucky," Shadow said, with a stern look. He picked a pistol from the window sill and placed it on his lap.

"Alright, no drama," Lucky replied with a shrug, slinging his rifle over his shoulder.

The second man looked on, not saying a word. He was dark, the colour of coal, with a scar above his left eye brow. Shadow looked in his direction. "Iron, get a seat for the lady. Lucky, did you get fuel for the generator?"

"I no see bike to carry me go. Besides, they said there is fuel scarcity as petrol marketers are on strike. So na black market dey sell."

Shadow hissed.

Iron brought a seat from the other side of the room. I collapsed into it and rested my aching legs. "Where is Dan?" I asked, looking around. The room was empty, save for the four of us. Lucky started humming a song. Iron looked away. Shadow kept a straight face, looking at me.

"Where is Dan?"

Shadow nodded in Lucky's direction and he left the room. I searched Iron's face for clues and found none. Several thoughts ran through my mind, all ending with the same question. Have they killed him?

I heard footsteps approaching and turned. A man entered the room, chains around his wrists. Lucky followed him, pointing his rifle at the man's neck. I couldn't make out his face from a distance but as he approached where I sat, the light from the kerosene lamp revealed a familiar face.

"Dan!" I sprang to my feet and ran to hug him.

After some time, Iron began pulling me away from Dan. "Reunion is over."

I held on to Dan. His shirt was dirty and he smelled like he had not bathed in a week. But I clung to him, especially after discovering that none of his fingers were missing.

"Love *nwantinti*! Love *na waya o*!" Lucky broke into a song.

Iron pulled us apart and I knelt in front of Shadow. "Thank you for not harming him. Thank you."

He smiled. "Dan has been useful to us here. He treats everyone, free of charge."

"He is our Doc!" Lucky chimed in.

"But he has missed his wedding," I pleaded. "His aged father is worried sick. Please, let him go."

Shadow smoked in silence, shifting his gaze from me to Dan. The smoke formed a cloud around his face. "Take them away."

Iron dragged me up from the ground amidst my struggles and led Dan and I away from the room. We entered a dark passage. He produced the flashlight and pointed in front of us. The ground was bare earth. We made a turn to the left and came face to face with a wooden door. He unlocked it and the door creaked open.

The smell hit me strong and hard: the smell of faeces mixed with that of stale urine. I covered my nose with my hands but soon uncovered it; I needed the air. There were murmurs in the room.

"Quiet!" Iron growled. "Bring your hands." He had brought a chain from a corner of the room and tied my wrists with it, securing it with a small padlock.

He shoved me forward. "You can sit anywhere."

His flashlight pointed at the corners of the room. I made out four figures sitting on the floor. "Can we get a light in here?" one of the figures said.

Iron left, throwing the room in total darkness.

"Let's sit here," Dan said. We were standing beside the door and with hands chained, we bent down, knelt and then lowered our buttocks to the ground.

We heard someone humming and unlocking the door. Lucky appeared and set a kerosene lamp at the center of the room. The wall bore our elongated, swaying shadows.

"Allow me to make some introductions." He stood near the light, hands clasped, his rifle hanging from his neck. His shadow loomed large on the wall behind him.

"The beautiful lady we have in our midst is Stella, Dan's bestie."

I turned my eyes to the floor. Some insects were circling the lamp.

"Stella, you already know Dan. The one at that corner, whimpering like a woman, is Agu. Next to him is Wale, then Stewart, and in that corner is Chief Okorodudu."

I couldn't see the faces of the men clearly but I noticed that Chief Okorodudu had a bandage on his left foot. Lucky turned to leave. "Behave yourselves. We try to treat you as well as we can because you are all assets. More than fifty million naira…"

The Chief cut him short. "But Dan paid. And yet, you refuse to release him. Instead, you kidnapped the person that brought the money. That's cruel. So, if my wife brings my ransom, will she be kidnapped and subjected to this inhumane treatment?"

"Shadow makes the rules. I don't. Besides, if we release Dan, who will be managing your diabetes? Eh? He is saving your life here. And we need you alive, at least till we get the money."

The Chief hissed as Lucky left.

I turned to Dan. "You shit and piss in here? Everyone?"

He nodded and pointed to a metal bucket in the corner. "They empty it once every three days. Terrible."

"Na wah o!"

Agu's loud whimpers filled the room.

"What's wrong with him?" I asked. "Why is he crying?"

Dan shook his head, and his reply made my jaw drop.

"It was his finger they cut and sent to Papa."

FIFTY-EIGHT

Streaks of light from the window signaled that it was morning. I had woken up at dawn hoping that the events of the previous day would turn out to be a nightmare. They were not. Mosquitoes had bitten my exposed forearms in many places, leaving swollen points of red skin that itched to no end.

A draft of air in the room brought the faecal smell to my nostrils. I retched. "This is just awful. Awful!"

Dan laughed. "When you stay here for more than a week, you won't notice the smell anymore. Thoughts of death and dying will preoccupy your mind."

I shook my head. "You know, I still don't get it. Why would someone want to kidnap you?"

"I can't say. I think I was unlucky. I had finished ward rounds that day and left for home, having been on call the previous night. I decided to take a short cut to avoid the usual traffic. I turned into a street and then noticed a jeep overtake me and suddenly two armed men jumped down. They ordered me to stop, pushed me out of the car and tied my hands. They collected my car keys and pushed me into the jeep. Chief Okorodudu was inside the car, tied up in the back seat."

"*Jesu!*"

He sighed. "It was just like a movie playing out. They blindfolded us and drove for a very long time. When we got here, they removed our blindfolds, chained us and pushed us into this room. Shadow told us to think up names of persons who could afford our ransom. They went out the next day and returned with Wale and Stewart. Agu and Gideon were brought in on the third day."

I looked around the room and did a quick count. "They released the person called Gideon?"

Dan shook his head, his face grim. "He's dead. He was trying to escape. Iron shot him in the head. He said it should serve as a warning to all of us."

Chief Okorodudu stirred in his sleep and continued his loud snoring.

"What's up with them?" I whispered to Dan, pointing at the others. "Their people never pay?"

He shrugged. "Hmmm. I heard Agu's brother refused to pay the two million naira that was requested. He told Shadow to go to hell."

"*Jesu*! Why nau?"

"Maybe he thought the call was a joke, that the whole kidnapping story was a ploy by Agu to extort money from him. So, Shadow cut Agu's finger to convince my father to pay."

"Stop mentioning my name there o! I am dying in pain here and you are busy calling my name!" Agu eased himself to a sitting position. "I will deal with you when I get out of here."

Dan struggled to his feet. "Please, let me take a look at that hand. I am afraid that it might get infected."

Agu was livid. "Don't you dare come near me!"

"Please."

"You no dey hear word? No come here."

Dan returned to my side and sat down.

Wale raised his head. "Agu, you still dey vex? Wetin happen don happen. No amount of anger can bring back your lost finger. Allow Dan to look at it."

Agu hissed. "You're just being stupid. Really."

"Who are you calling 'stupid'? Eh?"

Agu rose to his feet, his angry voice rousing Chief Okorodudu and Stewart from their sleep.

"Yeye bank manager that cannot raise ten million naira. Nonsense!" He was standing before Wale, who just smiled.

"I agree," Wale said. "I don't have ten million naira to my name. Bankers are not as rich as you guys think."

Agu hissed again and sat down in his corner. "Pesin go see una wear suit, drive big cars and speak big grammar, yet no shi-shi for pocket!"

Wale laughed. "Yes nau! All na packaging. Some bankers you see in suits earn less than a hundred thousand naira and work like slaves. So, don't envy them."

The solitary bulb hanging from the side of one of the room's walls came on. The glowing crescent within it shook as though it was hesitating.

"They've put on the generator," Chief Okorodudu said, sitting up. He walked to the bucket and started urinating. The faecal smell filled the room again and churned my stomach.

"Some of you bankers are rich, stupendously rich," the Chief continued as he zipped up his trousers after getting rid of every drop of urine. "My friend, a manager in one of the new generation banks, told me how they take fifty abi hundred naira from the bank accounts of customers, especially those with above hundred thousand naira in their accounts. The money disappears. No one asks questions. The customer doesn't even notice."

Wale raised his voice in protest. "Not every manager engages in such sharp practices."

"I didn't say you do such. If you did, you would have paid your ransom tey tey."

Everyone broke into laughter.

"What's so funny?" Iron was standing at the door, pistol in hand, looking around. No one spoke. He headed to where Stewart sat and dragged him up. "Phone time."

When they had left the room, I turned to Dan. "What's 'phone time'?"

"We all have specific times when Shadow calls our people or whoever he expects to pay our ransom. Stewart is 8am. I am 9am. Wale is 10am. Agu used to be 11am but they stopped giving him phone time when his brother swore not to pay…"

"Stop mentioning my name from your filthy mouth! I won't warn you again!" Agu fumed from where he sat.

"Calm down, Bros. *Kilode*?" Wale said, hitting his outstretched leg.

"I guess Chief is 12 noon," I said.

Dan nodded.

"Do they give you food here?"

Dan laughed at my question. "Technically, yes. Once a day. After phone time."

Agu sneered. "That one reach to call food? Rubbish tasteless bread with watery tea."

I shook my head. "Prison better pass this one."

"Seconded!" Chief Okorodudu said.

"Here no be Lagos State House of Assembly o!" Wale said, turning to him. "You na politician nau. Why haven't you paid your thirty million naira ransom?"

Chief shook his head. "My brother, nobody dey plan for this kain thing. We spend the money as it comes. I have told my wife to offset some of my assets to raise the money and get me out of here. I don't understand why she is dragging her feet."

"Women! Maybe she don already find better boyfriend while you're away," Agu said, laughing.

I couldn't understand Agu. Was his constant caustic jibes his own way of dealing with his pain or was he just a nasty person?

Chief shot him an angry look. "Stupid boy! You won't mind your business, abi?"

Just then, the door opened and Stewart walked in.

"How did it go?" Wale asked.

Stewart shook his head. "Could you believe that none of my fellow engineers at Shell could raise fifteen million to get me out of here? These are people I know that buy jeeps worth millions for their girlfriends."

I sighed.

"That guy Shadow is a good guy. Lucky is good, too." Stewart said, shaking his head. "It is Iron that has the heart of the devil."

Everyone stared at him. He walked to his spot beside Wale and sat. "They're all graduates. And tech-savvy. I helped them do some programming back there. We got talking."

"Graduates? Why are they kidnapping people up and down?" Chief asked, looking confused.

"No jobs. They've been jobless for five years and decided to take matters into their own hands. They deeply detest politicians. Iron was suggesting to Shadow that they kill Chief as it will send a message."

Chief was silent, his head bowed.

Stewart turned to Dan. "Do you think they will let us go after we bring the money?"

Dan shook his head. "I don't think they will."

FIFTY-NINE

"Something is terribly wrong," Chief Okorodudu said as Iron led him into the room. "She should have paid by now. Eh."

Iron kicked his rear and ordered him to sit, pointing a pistol to his head. "You think say we dey joke, abi? Bloody motherfucker! Na una wey keep this country as e dey so."

Chief Okorodudu was shaking where he sat. I saw a wet patch appear in his trousers.

Iron waved the pistol around. "All of una get luck say na Shadow dey run this show. We don get better offer to sell off your kidneys and livers to Malaysia and India for millions but Shadow still dey dull. See eh, una must pay o! Otherwise, we go sell una in pieces. A good kidney na two million naira for black market. Rubbish!"

He banged the door shut as he left and grumbled as he locked it. His voice came through the door as he walked away. "Make I see anybody wey go talk of food today. Idiots!"

Wale sighed as the footsteps had receded. "Na dry fasting today. Kai!"

Dan looked at me, his eyes welled up in tears. I remembered Victory and wondered if I was ever going to see her again. The thought of being butchered for my organs shook me to the core of my being and I broke down in sobs. Dan inched closer to me, his fingers reaching for mine. I grasped his hands despite the pain in my wrists from where the chains chaffed them.

"We will be fine, I promise," he said.

I looked into his eyes and searched for certainty. I found none.

In his side of the room, Chief Okorodudu fumed, banging his head on the wall. "I have assets worth over seventy million naira and my wife cannot raise thirty million to get me out of here?"

"No go wound yourself because of a woman," Agu said.

Stewart sighed. "Is there really any guarantee that we would be released when they get the money? Look at Dan."

"But she should make an effort. She doesn't sound disturbed on the phone. This is someone whose husband has been kidnapped for eleven days!" Chief struggled to his feet. "I am sending her home as soon as I get out of here."

"And marry one of your numerous mistresses?" Agu broke into laughter. "My brother, they are all the same thing."

I watched Chief as he walked to the bucket to urinate. The bandage on his left leg had turned brown. It shocked me that he wasn't limping. I turned to Dan. "He has a wound on his leg?"

Dan nodded. "Diabetic foot ulcer. It doesn't cause him pain because the nerves around that place are damaged. His legs are numb. Such ulcers take time to heal because the individuals keep hurting the spot unknowingly and the area has poor blood vessels to promote healing."

"Doc, Doc!" Stewart said, smiling. "My late landlord had such a sore on his leg. His doctor told him they have to amputate the leg. He refused. He died after a month."

Dan sighed. "The sore must have been infected. If he had agreed to the amputation, he would probably be alive up till now."

"Nobody is cutting my leg," Chief said, returning to his spot. "It's true I didn't manage my condition well till the ulcer appeared but since then I have been trying."

"Did Lucky give you your meds today?" Dan asked.

Chief shook his head. "They were angry after the call. They said no food for me today. Therefore, no drugs."

"Your dressing needs to be changed. I will speak to Shadow whenever I meet him."

Agu stood up and walked towards the bucket.

"Shit or piss?" Wale asked, a scowl on his face. "Shit." Agu removed his shorts and waved it over the bucket, causing the houseflies in it to scatter with a loud buzz. He sat on the bucket, stomping his legs alternately to scare off some stubborn flies. The bandage on his right hand was dirty, with yellow and brown stains. His palm was swollen.

"Wetin you chop wey you wan shit?" Chief asked, turning his face away. Agu strained, his lips pursed and his face contorted like that of a woman in labour.

I rose up and faced the window. It was covered with planks. I pressed my nose in the gaps between the planks to get some fresh air. I took a lungful and watched as a bird flew away from a nearby tree. I could make out two cars parked under the tree. One was Dan's Toyota Corolla and the other was a Lexus jeep. Beyond the tree was a stretch of barren land.

"We're in the middle of nowhere," I said, turning to Dan, who had stood up to stand beside me.

"I know." He turned and sat down.

"Have any of you thought of escaping from here?" I looked around the room.

Agu chuckled as he pulled up his shorts. "She don begin talk like Gideon. Dan, you no gist am?"

"Forget it," Dan said. "Gideon was smart, strong, and very intelligent. But he ended up dead. These people mean business."

I looked out of the window again. In the distance, I saw a cloud of dust rising. I turned to Dan. "A car is coming."

"That would be Lucky. He goes out with the cars to buy stuff."

As I watched the form of the car come into view, a surge of hope rose in me. "It is a police van!"

Everyone scrambled to the window and peeped through the gap. They reeked of stale sweat.

"It is a police van," Dan said. "One police van."

"My prayers have worked," Stewart said. "I knew God wouldn't let me die here."

I pressed my sweaty palms together as the white van approached. It veered off the road, close to the house.

"Where is it going?" Stewart asked, mopping his brow.

Minutes later, we heard the sound of a vehicle approaching and it appeared from behind the house and parked under the tree, close to the Lexus.

"There's only one man inside," Dan said, a frown on his face.

"Maybe the others still dey for road," Agu said. "They go soon reach."

Just then, Shadow appeared and walked to the van, holding a polythene bag. The door opened and a man in mufti came down. As he turned, my heart raced. I could not miss his light skin and curly hair.

"Sergeant Okoli!" I didn't know when his name escaped my lips. Dan pushed me away from the window to the ground. Everyone scattered to their spots, fear etched on their faces.

"Do you want to get us all killed?" Dan asked, in a hushed voice. "Recognizing anyone is an automatic death sentence."

"We don die already. Iron will walk in here and shoot all of us." Agu said, his chained wrists above his head.

My lips trembled as the reality of what I had seen hit me. The fact that a man I went to morgues with, combed Emergency rooms of hospitals with and planned a rescue with, was working with Shadow all along was mind-boggling. He was the secret to Shadow's omniscience. He was the insider.

We held our breaths and waited for the sounds of boots and the cocking of guns.

My stupidity had ruined everything.

SIXTY

We waited till dusk. "Maybe they didn't hear," Dan said, with a sigh.

"Or maybe dem dey wait for a perfect time to kill us. At night," Agu said.

I was still in shock. Sergeant Okoli had probably come to collect his own share of the loot. What made it worse was the fact that he knew how much we struggled to raise the money.

Chief turned to me. "How do you know the man?"

His question amused me. Know the man? The Sergeant Okoli I knew was different. And it was obvious I never really knew him. No one did. Except, perhaps, Shadow and his cohorts.

"He was the detective in charge of Dan's case."

Dan sat up, looking surprised. "Really?"

I nodded. "Everyone trusted him. The DPO assigned your case to him. We never suspected him."

Chief sighed. "Corruption has eaten into the fabric of our institutions. Imagine a police officer working hand in hand with kidnappers. Pathetic."

"This may be one of the reasons why most cases go unsolved. Corrupt officers on the payroll of criminals," Wale said with a shrug. "How do you think these people get their guns?"

We heard footsteps approach and sat still, our eyes on the door. Lucky entered carrying a polythene bag, followed by Iron and Shadow. They were dressed in military camouflage. Shadow had three black stars in the light brown space on his chest.

"Stand!" Iron hollered, cocking his rifle. My heart thumped.

"We are moving," Shadow said. "A few basic rules if you still love your life. You'll enter the cars and behave normally. If you try to play smart, behave funny or attract any attention, you'll pay."

Lucky emptied the contents of his bag. "Change of clothes for the men. Stella, you still look good."

As they walked us out of the room, my mind raced with possibilities. They needed at least two men in each car to maintain control. There were only three men. The one man in the second car could not be driving and wielding a gun at the same time. Maybe we could get a chance to overpower him.

My heart sank as I saw a lanky boy dressed in military uniform beside the Corolla. My escape plan had died a premature death.

"Musa, will drive the car. Iron, stay with him," Shadow said, grabbing my shoulder. He shoved me towards the Lexus. Chief and Wale joined us. Lucky brought up the rear. I turned to catch a glimpse of Dan, Agu and Stewart entering the Corolla with Iron.

Shadow got in the driver's seat and ordered me to enter in front. Wale and Chief clambered into the back of the Lexus and Lucky slammed the door shut. I heard him laugh and then felt the cold muzzle of a gun behind my neck. I didn't bother to turn.

The car reversed and the tinted glass was wound up. The air-conditioning unit blasted cold air. Shadow fiddled with the stereo knob till he got to a radio station playing highlife music. He nodded to the rhythm, seemingly oblivious of our discomfort.

"Put your wrists between your thighs," he said, and shot a glance at me as the car moved onto the expressway. I obeyed.

"Have you ever wondered why we don't bother to cover our faces or blindfold you?"

I shook my head, unsure of how to answer.

"Anyone?" he asked, tilting his head. No one spoke.

"Lucky, tell them."

Lucky's voice rose above the music. "Dead men don't tell tales."

"Simple."

Shadow's face was expressionless as he drove, his eyes as sharp as the headlamps illuminating the highway He drove with one hand, with the air of an expert at the wheel. Occasionally, he would look in my direction and give a smug smile which often disappeared as fast as it came.

We passed many police vans as we drove. Most had no occupants inside. Many checkpoints were deserted; we saw two policemen under a cashew tree, conversing. I was seething in anger as the car sped past and watched from the side mirror to see if they would turn. They didn't notice.

"Where are we going?" I had voiced out the question before I could stop myself. Lucky struck my neck with the muzzle of the gun. I felt a sharp pain and bent forward, a burning sensation moving from my neck to my head and down to my limbs.

Shadow laughed. "Calm down Lucky, she wants to know where we are going."

Lucky grunted. "She get mind."

"Lady, since you asked nicely, I will tell you."

He cleared his throat, all the while keeping his eyes on the road. "We have switched to Plan B. Your organs will be saving someone's life."

I recoiled in my seat. The heartlessness of it all riled me. "You mean that after bringing the five million naira you asked us to bring, this is how you repay us?"

He feigned pity. "Sorry, darling. See, we have a contract to supply twelve kidneys. When Gideon died from his stupidity, we were left with a problem. But you came along and balanced things out."

We neared a barricade on the road, made from barrels. A bush lamp burned on one of the barrels. The figures of two men stood in the distance, guns in one hand, waving. I felt the coldness of Lucky's gun disappear from the back of my neck.

As we approached, the headlamps made them out to be military men. Shadow slowed down and wound down the glass on his side. He flashed the weary-looking soldier a smile. "Captain Sabo. Heading to Dodan Barracks." The soldier threw a quick salute and gestured to him to pass.

"Shadow, there is trouble." Lucky's voice betrayed his panic.

From the side mirror, I saw that the Corolla had been stopped and Iron was out of the car, talking to the soldier who had just waved us through the checkpoint. I muttered a prayer of thanksgiving. Shadow pulled the car over.

"Shoot anyone that misbehaves," he said to Lucky before stepping out of the car. "They're more valuable dead now."

He slammed the driver's door and walked back to the checkpoint. I watched as he spoke to the soldier for some time, showing him a card from his breast pocket. He brought out Agu and showed the soldier his chained wrists. Agu fell to his knees, screaming. Iron slapped him and pushed him into the car. To my consternation, the soldier motioned them to get back in the car and move. I felt every strength in me ebb away.

Shadow entered the car, fuming. "Imagine, that stupid boy screaming to the soldiers that they've been kidnapped!"

"Kai! What did you say to them?" Lucky asked as soon as the car began to move.

"That they're political thugs that we want to teach a lesson at the barracks. That's why we chained them."

"And they bought it?" His voice could not hide his glee.

"Who would be stupid enough to doubt or disobey a higher-ranking officer? You wan die?"

"Guy, I dey gbadun your liver. Your confidence is extraordinary."

Shadow drove on in silence.

He turned the car into a bushy path. I looked at the side mirror and noticed the Corolla following us. The path was winding and lined with trees.

After some time, we emerged on a long stretch of untarred road. Through the side mirror, I could see the headlamps of the Corolla piercing the clouds of dust our car threw up as it sped along. My eyelids were heavy and I leaned back on the headrest.

A nudge from Lucky's gun woke me. The car was still, the engine revving. Shadow turned it off and we alighted. We were in a huge compound with two bungalows, surrounded by a tall fence. A small bulb gave off a yellow light from the wall. The two cars parked facing each other, their headlamps dispelling the surrounding darkness.

Musa came down from the Corolla and locked the gate.

"Bring me that bastard!" Shadow stormed towards the Corolla.

Iron pushed Agu forward and he fell on his knees, pleading.

"Please, please. I have a son. *Bikonu.* Please."

Shadow smiled. "You didn't remember that when you were screaming at the express." He turned to us. "How much more till you learn?"

I winced as three loud shots rang out from his pistol. Agu's lifeless body crashed to the ground, blood oozing from the gaping holes in his forehead, the red streams spilling onto the sand. I was rooted at the spot, frozen in morbid fear.

Shadow replaced his pistol and brought out his phone. "Alhaji, na Shadow. The twelve kidneys will be ready tomorrow and I am taking twenty-two million for all."

He put down the phone and looked around. "You've abused the freedom I gave you. From now on, you'll all be blindfolded and anyone that talks to the other will see my wrath. One of us will be with you at all times. This deal happens tomorrow and I won't have any of you ruin it. Nonsense!"

He turned to Dan. "Doc, assist our man inside to remove his two kidneys." He pointed at Agu's body. "Everything you need is inside the house."

Dan turned to look at me, his eyes saying everything I already knew.

Death was here.

SIXTY-ONE

We were led into an empty room. The ground was covered with a red carpet and two bulbs glowed from the green walls, opposite each other. The single window had dusty louvers and the burglary proof bars on the inside looked formidable.

"Sit!"

Our buttocks hit the floor at the sound of Iron's voice. The image of Agu's lifeless eyes was stuck in my mind. He may have been tactless, but he didn't deserve death.

Iron faced Dan. "Remove your shirt." Dan obeyed.

Setting his rifle down, Iron tore the shirts to pieces. He then asked Dan to step aside. Taking the pieces one by one, he blindfolded Wale, Stewart and Chief. He took a piece and stood in front of me, a smirk on his face.

"Turn around." I turned and in an instant, my eyes were covered.

"Lucky, you will remain with them. I am leaving with Doc to collect the kidneys from that bastard. Any one wey do '*pim*', blow his brains out. Idiots!"

I heard footsteps and then the door slammed shut. Another set of footsteps began to walk the length and breadth of the room. "If any of una wan piss or shit, tell me." Lucky informed us. "There is a toilet in the next room."

"I wan piss. Abeg." It was Chief's voice.

"Already?"

There were sounds of shuffling feet and then a door opening. It was followed by the sound of liquid trickling into a cistern. There was a flushing sound, and footsteps.

In the ensuing silence, I grappled with the numerous questions on my mind. How does it feel to be cut open and have one's organs removed? I heard stories of persons who sold theirs in exchange for large sums of money. I had never heard of one's organs taken against their will. Was it because the victims didn't survive it?

I thought of death and dying. What was it like in those few moments before a gunshot to the head? If I were in Agu's shoes, would I have begged for my life or remained resolute and flint-faced? Would my death be fast like Agu's or slow and protracted, with unbearable pain? And who would pull the trigger?

I felt trickles of urine escape from between my thighs.

"I want to urinate," I said, raising my voice.

Lucky approached and pulled off my blindfold. He led me to the toilet, a small cubicle attached to the room. The wall had white tiles on them and the floor was cemented. I struggled with my chained hands to unzip my jean trousers. Lucky laid his rifle next to the wall and helped me. Then he turned around, back to me, as I pulled the trousers to my knees. I pulled my panties down and sat on the bowl, relieved as a stream of urine left me.

"So, how does it feel doing what you do?" I asked him. It was an unplanned question. I figured since we were going to die, it wouldn't hurt having final conversations.

The response came faster than I expected. "Shut up!"

I remained on the bowl even after the urine had stopped coming. He tapped his foot on the ground. "It's midnight. Nine more hours and we'll be done," he said.

Was this information for me? And why was he sounding so sad?

"I don suffer, mehn. I don suffer!" He paced from wall to wall.

I didn't know what to make of what I was hearing. Was this panic, anger or both?

I felt the urge to say something and I did.

"You're not alone. I sheltered a stranger and got HIV in return." After the words left my lips, it struck me how ridiculous it sounded.

"You dey HIV positive?"

"Yes."

"Ah! I no think say we go need your kidney," he said, shaking his head. "But, I no fit tell Shadow. He go kill me for talking with you." He let out a heavy sigh. "We don kill two people now. Two!"

"It is not your fault." I said, rising from the bowl. "You can still stop this."

"It's too late. Abeg, stop talking. Or you become the third dead body."

I swallowed the rest of my words as I pulled up my jeans, his last statement reverberating in my head.

He led me into the room and replaced my blindfold. I sank to the ground, listening as his footsteps went from one end of the room to another. I wondered what was going on in his mind, the amount of societal pressure that had pushed him into kidnap and murder. He must have seen his friends get rich

234 | Kelvin Alaneme

overnight, secondary school dropouts who pulled up in the latest SUVs. He must have seen them build houses, marry wives and run businesses. As a broke graduate, he was still combing the streets of Lagos for a miracle, searching for a job. He was the ultimate prey. The hunted ones were now hunting and killing the innocent.

"Stella." Dan's voice woke me. I had dozed off, overpowered by the turmoil in my heart. I turned my head in the direction of his voice. There was a strong smell of fresh blood coming from him.

"Shhh!" I figured one of the men might hear him.

"Lucky stepped out. The worst is already here. That call Shadow made? He wasn't bluffing. They're taking our kidneys in less than four hours."

I sighed. "To think you might be the one to cut me open."

"They invited a surgeon within their racket. He has a nurse with him. They're taking my kidneys too." His voice sounded grim. "They have a mini operation theatre back there, complete with flasks filled with ice for preserving the organs."

He paused, then continued. "I feel terrible for putting you through this stress, Stella."

I groped around till my hands touched his. "Don't worry. Whatever the outcome, just know that we did what we could."

We heard footsteps approaching and I withdrew my hands. The footsteps stopped in front of where I sat.

"Stand, you two!" It was Lucky's voice. "It is time. Na una go be the first to die."

My heart pounded as he removed my blindfold.

"Please," I muttered. "Please."

He shoved me towards the door and stepped back to untie Dan's eyes. Dan followed without a word.

I took one last look at the room. The others sat in silence, eyes covered, hands clasped. Chief's lips were quivering. Lucky pushed me outside the room.

We went through a passage and came to a part of the compound illuminated by a bulb. Roosters crowed in the distance as I took in the damp early morning fresh air.

"Keep moving!"

We did not know where we were headed. As we got to the edge of the fence, we stopped short of a small gate which was locked.

"Kneel. Put your hands on your heads."

We fell on our knees, my lips parting in prayer. Dan looked at me. There was despair in his eyes.

"Say some prayers." Lucky raised his rifle and cocked.

I closed my eyes and prayed for Victory, for Uche and especially for Old Major. I knew our deaths would crush them. My prayers drifted to Dan and me. We did not deserve the death staring us in the face. Yet, at that point, I felt peace. A wave of tranquility filled my heart and I began to hum a hymn.

I heard a creaking sound and opened my eyes. The small gate was open and Lucky held the unlocked padlock in his hands. Producing a bunch of keys from his trouser pockets, he unlocked the chains on our wrists.

He turned to me. "I think wetin you talk. To be honest, I no know wetin I dey do right now. E fit no dey enough to wash off the blood stains but this is a start. Everything ends now."

I stared at him, shocked by his actions. He gave me a smile. It was bizarre on that face. I hugged him, despite the rifle between us. "Thank you."

His hands trembled as he shoved us outside the gate. "Run!"

We broke into a barefoot run. The damp morning air caressed our faces as we leapt through the bush, tearing down obstructing leaves with our hands. We stumbled upon a road and stopped, panting and out of breath. In the distance, staccato gunfire shattered the silence of the young morning.

Summoning every ounce of energy within me, I followed Dan's lead and fled into a nearby bush.

SIXTY-TWO

People stared at us as we ran past. Fishermen returning from the river, their fish-laden nets slung over their shoulders, naked children being bathed by their mothers, a group of women threshing corn by the roadside. Seeing two strangers - the male, shirtless and the female, hysterical - running at top speed, must have been jarring.

When the early morning darkness lifted, it dawned on us that we were in a village. We came to a clearing that housed empty stalls roofed with thatch. Dan slowed down and stopped beside one stall, panting. I slumped to the ground, exhausted.

"Where are we?" I was struggling to catch my breath.

He looked around. "I don't know."

"Do you think they are after us?"

"I don't know. But we have to find somewhere to hide."

I was too tired to get up. "Let's rest for some time. My legs are sore."

"Those gunshots?"

"I don't know."

For a moment, I wondered what Shadow would do to Lucky if he found out he released us and what fate awaited the others. I pictured Shadow's rage and felt a deluge of pity for them, especially Wale and Stewart. These were smart, young people who did not deserve their predicament.

An old woman with a basket of vegetables on her head walked past, her frail body covered in a yellow wrapper. Dan ran after her. "Excuse me, Ma."

She doubled her pace, oblivious to his call. He ran in front of her, making her stop in her tracks. She looked at him, apparently confused.

"Where is this village? We are kind of lost."

The woman shook her head.

"Speak Yoruba for her," I said, approaching where they stood.

"*Nibo ni abule yi wa? A ti sonu!*"

The woman broke into a smile and spoke in a strange language. Dan looked in my direction and I shook my head. She did not understand us.

We trekked from the square and followed a small bushy trail. The path went downhill and near its end we could hear people's voices. It ended at the bank of a stream. Its murky water flowed westward and some young men were swimming at the deep end. Their clothes were strewn on the wet ground and they looked in our direction as we approached.

"Does anyone here speak English?" Dan shouted as their heads appeared above the water.

The boys murmured for some time. One of them waded across to where we stood, his wet shorts clinging to his skin. He looked no older than twelve.

"I go to school at Community Grammar School."

"Good boy," Dan said, rubbing the boy's wet hair with his hand.

"Where is this town?"

The boy stared at us as though wondering what to think of the question.

"We are lost," I said. "Where is this?"

"Ajara Topa, this village."

"Ajara Topa?" Dan scratched his head. "We want to get to Lagos."

"I never go. I never leave Ajara Topa or Badagry sef."

I turned to Dan. "We are in Badagry?"

"It appears so."

Some of the boys in the water called out to the boy. He ignored them.

Dan placed a hand on his shoulder. "Where can we make a phone call? Telephone."

"Telephone. My father makes telephone call in front of our house."

"Please, take us to him."

The boy appeared hesitant and cast a glance at his friends in the water.

"We will give you money," I said.

He sorted through the pile of clothes at our feet, selected a blue checkered shirt and in a trot, led us up the bushy path, shrugging his shirt on.

We stopped at an unpainted house. In front of the house, there was a big yellow umbrella attached to a white table. Used recharge cards were pinned around the umbrella and they twirled in the morning breeze. A man sat at the table and dropped the three phones in his hands as we approached.

"Papa hear only Egun," the boy said, looking at us.

The man began to speak to the boy in their language. The boy replied, all the while pointing to Dan. The man's face turned sympathetic.

"Telephone." He handed Dan an old Nokia phone.

"Who are you calling?" I asked.

"Old Major and Bola. They're the only numbers I have in my memory, apart from yours."

I hit his arm and he smiled. It was a genuine smile - the first I had seen on his face in days.

He pressed the phone's buttons and held it to his ear. I looked around. Across the road, a small he-goat was chasing a larger she-goat at top speed. It caught up with it and without warning, mounted its rear.

"Old Major is not picking up."

"Why?"

"I have tried three times."

"Maybe this whole kidnap thing has made him stop picking calls from strange numbers. Try Bola."

I watched his face as he punched the keys.

"Ah, Bola. Thank God! Yes, it is me."

He placed the phone on loudspeaker mode. I heard some commotion in the background, sounds of people shouting.

"How is Stella?" Bola asked, after shouting for a few seconds. "Old Major has been worried. They admitted him into the hospital. The doctor said his blood pressure was through the roof."

"Stella is fine. She is here with me. How is Papa?"

"He was fine this morning. I believe this good news will make him bounce back. Where are you?"

"Somewhere in Badagry. Ajara Topa village. Our escape was a miracle. They may still be after us, so we need to get out of this place as soon as possible."

"Ok. I will charter a cab and head down there. Do they have anything like a motor park?"

"Bola, we are avoiding public places right now. The people here barely understand English. We are in front of an unpainted building where people make calls. It has a huge yellow umbrella in front."

"Ok. Just wait there. I am coming right away. My regards to Stella. God! We've been through hell these past two weeks."

After the call, the boy served as our intermediary with the father, relaying our predicament to the man the best way he could. When he finished speaking, the man sprang to his feet and dragged us by the hand into the building. His panic amused us.

Dan turned to the boy. "Tell your father that the armed men are not close."

The boy relayed the information to the man and he stood still, looking confused.

"Tell him we would still need to hide in his house and we will need to keep this phone with us."

I felt some rumblings in my stomach. "Tell him we also need food and water."

The man led us into a living room, using gestures to urge us to sit down before leaving us. He returned after some time with a long loaf of bread and two bottles of Coca-Cola. I grabbed one of the bottles and opened it with my teeth. In an instant, the bottle was empty. As I set it down, I noticed the man watching me and shaking his head. I turned to Dan. His bottle was also empty. "This man doesn't know that we haven't eaten anything for close to three days."

The man left the room and returned with an old orange shirt which he handed to Dan.

Dan tore the loaf in two and handed me one half. "What will we eat the bread with?"

"You're still asking questions," I said, chewing a mouthful.

The boy entered the room with water in two enamel cups. Such thoughtfulness. "Chai. Thank you," I said.

"What's your name?" Dan asked him as he turned to leave.

"Osete."

"Osete, you're a good boy. You're a blessed child. Thank you."

The boy's face lit up and he ran out of the room, smiling.

"What's the time now?" I asked.

Dan looked at the phone. "9.32am." He shook his head. "I woke up thinking this day would end differently but here we are."

Bola called by 11.40am. "Our cab has entered Badagry," She informed us. "A red cab. We are driving towards Ajara town. The driver knows Ajara Topa village and he said it is still far off."

"That's great. We are waiting."

"Your father wants to speak with you."

Dan had a look of relief on his face. "You're with him?"

"Daniel, *nwa m*. My son!" Old Major's voice came over the phone. He sounded weak, and my heart filled with sorrow at the thought of what he'd been through. "I heard the good news."

"Papa. How're you? I heard you were at the hospital."

"Hmmm. These people nearly killed me. How's Stella?"

I took the phone from Dan's hand. "I am here, Papa. God just saved us."

"We thank and bless His Holy Name. When Bola came to the hospital to inform me this morning, I told the doctor that I was leaving. That I must go to see my son. And my daughter."

Dan took the phone. "We will talk well when you get here. Just ask for places where they make phone calls in the village. We will wait for you in front of the house."

We sat on some cement blocks outside the building, looking out into the distance. Villagers passed on their bicycles, farm produce tied on the carriers. Three young women passed, earthenware pots balanced on their heads. They discussed in loud voices and Dan's eyes followed their swaying hips.

I tapped his shoulder. "Concentrate."

He let out a loud laugh. "Mind your business joor."

Dan was the first to see the dust rising in the distance. "Look."

The bonnet of a car appeared, growing bigger as it came close.

"A red car," I said, squinting. "It should be them."

The car pulled up in front of the house. Old Major jumped out, his arms outstretched as we ran to him. "My children are safe!"

Bola joined in the hug and gave Dan a kiss. "God has shamed the devil," she said, tears of joy running down her face.

Osete and his father watched the drama with smiles on their faces.

I turned to Old Major. "Papa, you need to thank this boy and his father. They've been wonderful."

Old Major brought out some money, counted ten one thousand naira notes and gave it to the boy. Osete handed the money to his father who shook his head, speaking in their native tongue.

"Papa say no." The boy handed the money back to Old Major.

"Okay. Keep the money for your schooling," Dan said.

The boy shook his head. "Papa say no. Help, free."

His words brought tears to my eyes. I drew him close and hugged him. Bola insisted we take a photograph with them before we left. Osete stood next to me, grinning as the cab driver took the picture with Bola's phone.

We bade Osete and his father goodbye and got into the cab. Dan sat at the back between Bola and I.

As we drove off, I looked back. Osete was standing in the middle of the road, waving.

I put my hand out the window and waved till he disappeared into the distance.

SIXTY-THREE

Old Major's face turned pale when we told him about Sergeant Okoli. "You mean he was working with the boys all this time?" He was looking back at us from the front seat. I nodded.

"And he is still walking around, free?" Bola threw a fist at the back of the front seat.

"I don't think he knows that we saw him. But the boys may have told him of our escape," Dan said.

"In that case, it is unsafe to hang around the house," Old Major said, shaking his head.

"He knows my house," I said, my blood running cold as I remembered that he had dropped me off at my home. Sergeant Okoli had made Lagos a risk for me too.

Dan turned to me. "We will lay low in a guest house around your area today and figure things out."

My shaking hands betrayed my unease. "I need to get home to my daughter. I haven't seen her in days."

Bola brought out her phone. "My Senior Partner knows the Commissioner of Police. I'll make some calls and we will see to it that the man is arrested."

"I will go straight to his DPO," Old Major said. "This is despicable!"

The car stopped in front of my compound. Mama Tunde was mixing feed for her roosters as we entered. She straightened up when she saw me, a delighted smile on her face. "Ah, Stella! Long time, no see." She greeted Dan, Old Major and Bola, then turned back to me, a frown creasing her brow as she took in my unkempt look. "What happened? Why do you look like this?"

"It's a long story, Ma. But I am back now."

"Okay o! E good as you don come back. Victory no gree play with my children o, crying for her mother. Every morning wey she dey go school, na so so cry cry. I no sure say she gree go today. Nkechi no drop key so she suppose dey house…"

I thanked her and hurried up the stairs, Dan and the others following me. I knocked on the door, overwhelmed by a feeling of gratitude.

Nkechi answered the door and froze on seeing me. "Stella!" She hugged me as she shouted. "Victory, Mummy is back!"

Victory emerged from the room, dressed in her school uniform, her eyes wide in disbelief. I detached myself from Nkechi's grip and lifted her up, planting several kisses on her tear-streaked face.

"When you didn't return, I went to the address you gave me at Amuwo-Odofin. When Dan's dad told me you didn't come back. I lost it." Nkechi said.

"She punched me o!" Old Major said, laughing.

"I didn't know what to tell Victory. Today, she refused to go to school, screaming that she wants her mummy."

We all laughed as well. Dan carried Victory, throwing her up in the air and catching her. "You're now a big girl. Very heavy." Victory giggled. Bola and Old Major sat on the sofa, watching them.

I took Nkechi into the room.

"What happened?" She asked.

"It is a long story. But God saved us. I was kidnapped by the same group when I went to drop the ransom. They weren't just your normal everyday kidnappers. These boys harvest and sell human organs at the black market. And they have someone in the police working with them."

"Eh ehn?" Nkechi snapped her fingers.

"I may be leaving Lagos for good. Relocate somewhere else. We will be staying at a Guest House tonight. Old Major said we will be traveling tomorrow to his village, in Orlu. We will lie low for some time till we figure things out."

"What will happen to your shop?"

"I don't know, can you help me supervise? Pay yourself a salary. This house… I've only just renewed the rent, you can stay here until it is due and help me renew it for next year."

She smiled and hugged me. "I know you will need all the money you can get. But we can talk about all this later. For now, you just need to be safe. I will miss you, big sister."

Just before we entered the living room, she drew me back by the hand. I turned.

"Dan and Bola," she whispered. "Are they still getting married?"

"Why not? They just need to set a new date, that's all."

I remembered my antiretroviral drugs which I had missed for three days and fished them out from my dresser, then went to the kitchen. I poured a glass of water and took them.

Nkechi served us a meal of jollof rice and chicken. I devoured the meal and in minutes scraped the last grains from my plate. I sank my teeth into the chicken.

"My God," I moaned.

Bola laughed as I chewed the bones.

It felt good to be home.

SIXTY-FOUR

We went to a guest house at the end of my street. It was secluded and nondescript with no signposts announcing its existence. We checked out their rooms and paid for three. I stayed in the one assigned to me, playing with Victory. Dan was with Bola in the next room and Old Major had left his room for the Police Station.

I held Victory's hands. "We will be traveling." Her countenance did not change. It was obvious she did not understand, or even care. All that mattered to her was that we were together. And I never planned to leave her side again.

That evening, Old Major came into our room, followed closely by the DPO, Dan and Bola. The DPO sat in the only seat in the room, facing away from the table. The others sat on the bed.

"I must start by saying that I'm glad both of you are alive to tell this story. This evening, I got a call from the Commissioner of Police urging me to look into a complaint he got regarding my chief detective, Sergeant Okoli. That was before your visit." He looked in Old Major's direction. "I have followed this case since it was reported at the station. I was a detective myself and rose through the ranks. I came to get your testimony. The officer in question will be arrested and a detailed investigation carried out. If he is found complicit, then he will face the music in the court of law." He put on his tape-recorder, stopping from time to time to jot into his writing pad as we narrated our ordeal.

By the time we were done, he struggled to find his voice. "I am deeply sorry for what you've been through. On behalf of the Force, I apologize for the wrongs done by the erring officer. I would suggest you lie low through all this. The kidnappers are still at large. Every measure of caution should be taken."

I slept well that night, covered in the soft duvet the guest house provided, with Victory in my arms. She woke me twice to take her to urinate but I fell asleep as soon as my body hit the bed upon our return each time.

Nkechi knocked on the door around 6am. I had just finished bathing Victory and was dressing her up.

"I packed what I could," she said, dropping two bags on the ground. "The clothes should last you for a while. Bras, underwear, everything is there. Victory's clothes are there too."

"Thank you. Do look in at the shop from time to time. Tell Ebele she is in charge now. She should render the shop accounts to you. I'll come and see them when all this is over."

She nodded and hugged me. "Safe journey," she whispered.

She turned and lifted Victory. "My Queen, I will come and see you one day, you hear?" Victory flashed a smile and nodded.

"Where is Bola?" I asked as we checked out of the guest house with our luggage.

Dan sighed. "She is not coming with us due to her work. It will be selfish of me to ask her to drop her hard-earned career and go on the run with me."

He had a point. However, for a couple about to start a family together, I felt staying apart was not the best. "Both of you are getting married. I think you should be together at the same place. It's so unfortunate that all this happened."

We boarded a taxi to take us to the park. Old Major was also traveling with us.

"Will you be coming back to Lagos?" I asked him, as the bus left the park an hour later.

"To come and do what? I have sold my two shops. I am now officially retired and tired."

Dan laughed. "Soldiers are never tired, especially the old ones. Maybe one day you'll run for President."

Old Major hissed. "Keep dreaming, boy. Keep dreaming."

SIXTY-FIVE

Orlu had the serenity of an ancient town. The roads were free, the people smiled and life happened in slow motion. We entered Old Major's village home, a modest bungalow perched at the corner of a large, fenced compound. A coconut tree stood in the middle of the courtyard and had littered the ground with brown coconuts. Some grasses had grown close to the fence and the dusty windows testified to prolonged absence.

"Welcome to our little abode," Old Major said as he pushed the gate open.

I smiled. Victory stopped to kick one of the coconuts lying on the ground.

"It is not a ball, darling," I called out, stopping to lift her into my arms. Two of Dan's cousins came around and joined him in bringing in our bags.

Life in Orlu had its perks. I enjoyed the fact that no one knew me. Old Major told everyone who asked that I was his daughter and I smiled as their eyebrows went up in confusion. I had ruled out going to my village because of Victory. My people frowned at childbirth outside wedlock and I wasn't ready to answer many unsolicited questions.

The following week, Dan accompanied Victory and I to the newly established Teaching Hospital to register at the HIV Clinic. They tested Victory again for the virus. She was negative. I was the last on the line.

"Stella Okoro." The nurse that called my name pointed to the doctor's office. Dan took Victory from me and I walked to the steel door.

The doctor was a balding middle-aged man with a huge smile. "I am Dr. Sogunro. Sit, please."

I sat opposite the table as he leafed through my folder.

"How long have you been taking the antiretrovirals?"

"Just over four years."

He smiled. "You haven't missed a day?"

"Well, I missed three days. A week ago. My medications were not with me."

He frowned. "Why? You should take them along when you travel."

"I didn't travel, Sir. I was kidnapped."

He leaned back in his seat and adjusted his ward coat. "Tell me what happened."

In the space of an hour, I emptied my life's story on his consultation desk, amidst sobs. Jide, Victory, Lagos, the kidnapping, Dan. By the time I was done, he was standing, hands on his head.

"Wow," he said, dabbing his eyes with a white handkerchief. "I work with the National Agency for the Control of AIDS, NACA, for short. Your story is powerful. I would love the world to hear your message."

I stared at him. He glanced at the clock and wrote my prescription inside the folder. Then, he gave me his card and collected my phone number on a sheet of paper.

"What took so long?" Dan asked as I came out of the office.

I smiled. "We were telling stories."

After I had picked up my medications, we met Dr. Sogunro outside as we were leaving.

"Dan?" He turned to me, while shaking Dan's hand. I nodded. Dan looked at him, surprised. "And this must be Victory," the doctor added, touching Victory's cheeks.

He placed his hand on Dan's shoulder. "Stella told me everything. I am glad you are safe. Have you found a place to work yet?"

"I'm still searching," Dan said.

"Meet me tomorrow by 9am. I will take you to the Chief Medical Director and see if there is an opening for a medical officer."

Dan took his hand with glee. "Thank you, Sir. I appreciate this, Sir."

The following week, Dan got a call to come to the hospital and pick up his appointment letter. He came home with the letter and danced around the compound.

That night, as I was dressing Victory up for bed, Dan entered the room. He banged the door shut behind him.

"What's wrong?" I asked, startled.

He paced the room for some time. "It's Bola. We agreed that if I get a new job, she would relocate. I called to tell her about the job with the Teaching Hospital. She didn't sound happy. When I inquired, she told me she cannot leave Lagos. That she has invested too much in her firm to leave. She talked of travelling abroad later this year for her Masters. Can you imagine that?"

"I am sure both of you will work something out," I said. "Don't get yourself worked up, okay?"

"She is just being selfish. Selfish." He banged the door again as he left.

Old Major's voice trailed the loud noise. "Break down the doors, *inugo*?"

I called Bola the following evening.

"What's the problem?" I asked as her voice came on the line. "Dan has refused to eat and walks around all day looking morose."

"There's no problem. I just told him I can't leave Lagos. I don't understand why he is afraid to come back, especially now that those kidnappers have been caught."

"They've been caught? When?"

"Two days ago. Sergeant Okoli, after he was arrested, helped the officers round them up. Their faces are in the dailies. The fair one and the dark one with a scar on his face."

"Shadow and Iron! Just the two of them?"

"Yes. They were caught with many army uniforms and various assault rifles."

I sighed. "Thank God!"

An awkward stretch of silence followed.

"Have a nice evening, Stella." The line went dead with a click.

Later that evening, Dan entered the room with some news. "They've found my car, close to Seme border. The DPO called me this afternoon. The boys have been arrested."

"That's great." I walked to the door where he stood. "Did they find the others? Chief, Wale, Stewart?"

He sighed. "The Police recovered their bodies in a shallow grave beside the house, including Lucky's.

Shadow and Iron confessed to shooting everyone in a fit of rage. The Alhaji was also arrested."

I felt my heart swell with sadness, punctuated by harrowing guilt. Would the others have still been alive if we hadn't escaped? There was no way to tell.

Dan placed a hand on my shoulder. "It could have been us in that grave but for divine providence. We should justify our freedom by living well, soaking up every moment and taking nothing for granted."

I nodded, still overcome with grief. "They'll all rot in hell, those boys. As well as Sergeant Okoli and anyone connected with them. Devils."

After we had eaten dinner, I called Dan aside. "I spoke to Bola this evening."

"What did she say?"

"Same thing you told me."

"They want me back in Lagos to pick up the car. I will resolve every issue with Bola while I am there."

That night, I was in the same recurring dream I've had most nights since we escaped from captivity. In the dream, I knelt in front of Shadow, the barrel of his pistol on my forehead.

"Confess," he said.

"To what?" I asked, willing him to get it over with.

Every night, he pulled the trigger, the sound of the gunshot rousing me.

I would wake up panting, drenched in sweat.

That night, as he pulled the trigger, all I heard was an empty click.

SIXTY-SIX

August 20, 2016.

A man in flowing *agbada* was speaking at the podium. The stage was decorated in red and on the backdrop, a projected image showed graphs and charts of the number of people living with HIV in the various states of Nigeria. An air-conditioning vent above me sent blasts of cold air down, sprinkling my skin with goose-flesh. The hall was full and many government officials sat at the table on the stage.

Victory was seated beside Dan and looked mesmerized by the man speaking.

"Here, cover yourself with this," Dan said, handing me his jacket.

I collected it with a grateful smile. "Thank you."

The previous year had been the busiest year of my life. I toured many cities in Nigeria with Dr. Sogunro, creating awareness on HIV/AIDS and sharing my story. The response was overwhelming. NACA made me an Ambassador and I received a series of training on counseling and testing. I was interviewed by many newspaper houses and shared my story on television a couple of times.

"We will be in Abuja on the 1st of December," Dr. Sogunro had told me as I locked up my small office at the hospital.

"Next week?"

He nodded, smiling. "World AIDS Day. NACA is organizing a big event. People from UNAIDS will be there."

I felt uneasy whenever he announced a trip. I hated flying. Clutching my seat belt with sweaty palms, I stayed as still as possible from takeoff till the plane touched down at our destination. My heart skipped whenever anyone stood up and walked around while we were in the air. I feared their movement could make the plane topple out of the sky.

"You're going," Dr. Sogunro insisted. "And you can bring two people."

I begged Dan to accompany me on the trip. He had been my pillar of support and helped me handle the backlash I faced from a handful of persons who reacted negatively on hearing or reading my story.

"No one can make you feel inferior without your consent," he said one day as I lamented about the snide remarks and lingering stares. "You're better than most of them. You own your story and have made something out of nothing. It's important that we all share our stories like you are sharing yours."

"But I don't have a degree. I am practically a nobody. Why should I be the one telling this story?"

He smiled. "Why shouldn't it be you? It's your story and you are the most qualified to tell it. Besides, as more and more people relate with your story, it transforms from 'your story' to 'our story'. By deciding to share this story, you've become a mouthpiece for many, lending words to their daily experiences."

I hugged him. His words were all the push I needed.

Bola had called off the engagement and moved abroad for her Master's degree. Dan was shattered. I tried to console him as much as I could.

"You will find love again," I said, whenever I saw him staring into an empty space. "I guarantee it."

He would respond with a smile. "You can't guarantee something as fickle as love."

Dan's jacket gave me the much needed warmth. I had been afraid of seeming unsophisticated and was ready to bear the cold, but he had helped me out.

The Minister of Health was reading an address. His voice was sonorous and I loved the way he pronounced words. "We must crush HIV. We must make more people aware." There was resounding applause following the Minister's speech. The Director of NACA mounted the podium to hand out the Award of Excellence.

"The Award of Excellence this year goes to an indefatigable crusader. A man, whose hard work and efficiency in coordinating teams is instrumental to the success we are recording in the campaign today. Dr. Ebenezer Sogunro!"

I jumped up from my seat, screaming and clapping. Dr. Sogunro mounted the stage with his wife and son to receive the award.

Just then, Victory left her seat beside Dan and came to me. I frowned, as I had told her not to move around, and lifted her to my lap. "Clap. Clap. Our friend got the award," I said to her. I noticed her fists were clenched. "What are you holding?"

She opened her left hand. It took me a moment to realize what I was staring at. A ring. A silver ring with a beautiful side stone.

In my daughter's right hand was a piece of paper. My heart pounded as I opened it. Scrawled in her handwriting were five words. *Will you marry Uncle Dan?*

I turned. Dan was on one knee, smiling.

"Stella Okoro." I heard my voice over the loudspeakers and turned to the podium. The Minister was holding the microphone and looking around. "The new UNAIDS Ambassador for Africa is Miss Stella Okoro. Come up to the stage for recognition."

I felt dizzy as I stood up to a standing ovation. My world was spinning so fast and I was submerged in a deluge of emotions. I slipped on the ring and stepped away from my seat, still trying to understand how everything seemed to be happening at this moment. It felt like I'd been hit by a truck - a truck of good fortune.

"Is that a 'Yes'?" Dan asked as I handed him the jacket.

I nodded, blew him a kiss and walked to the stage, bidding my mind to steady its lenses and capture this image in one lasting frame: a young, scarred woman in a black sequin gown, wearing a big smile and walking on the threshold of a bright new beginning.

As I shook the Minister's hand amidst cheers from the audience, I paused to take a deep breath.

The air smelled like redemption.